MORT DRUCKER'S MAD SHOW-STOPPERS

A MAD BIG BOOK

A MAD BIG BOOK

Copyright © 1967, 1968, 1969, 1970, 1971,
1972, 1973, 1974, 1975, 1976, 1977, 1978, 1979,
1980, 1981, 1982, 1983, 1984, and 1985
by E.C. Publications, Inc.

Mort Drucker on Caricature Copyright 1973
Excerpt from "The Art of Humorous Illustration"
Watson Guptil Publishers

All rights reserved. No part of this book may be reproduced
without permission. For information address E.C. Publications, Inc.,
485 Madison Avenue, New York, N.Y. 10022.

Title "MAD" used with permission of its owner,
E.C. Publications, Inc.

This **MAD BIG BOOK** is published by
arrangement with E.C. Publications, Inc.

Printed in the United States of America

First Printing: June 1985
10 9 8 7 6 5 4 3 2 1

CONTENTS

The Oddfather 4

Mort Drucker On Caricature 13

The Oddfather Part Too 14

Flopeye 22

Mad Cover # 225 29

The Clods of '44 30

The Sam Pebbles 37

Abominal House 42

True Fat 50

Raving Bully 56

Cease 64

Brother Hoods 71

Dullus 78

Mad's X-Rated Celebrity Trivia Quiz 85

Catch-All 22 86

Antenna on the Roof 92

Mad Cover # 176 99

What's the Connection? 100

Being Not All There 108

Alias 116

Midnight Wowboy 124

Mad Cover # 169 131

The Shootiest 132

Jaw'd 138

Jaw'd Too 146

Rockhead 154

THE FAMILY THAT PREYS TOGETHER SLAYS TOGETHER DEPT.

Hey, Gang! Tired of all the garbage they're showing on motion picture screens lately? Well, here's a "Family" film for a change! And now, meet the "Family":

This is Don Vino Minestrone. Not too long ago, he was just a poor immigrant from Sicily. Now he's a leading racketeer, extortionist and killer. How did Don Vino get where he is today? By putting his faith in The American Way of Life.

Here's Mama Minestrone, a typical lovable Sicilian housewife. It seems like only yesterday at another wedding that Mama herself said, "I do!" Come to think of it, that was the last time she opened her mouth.

This is Don Vino's daughter, Canny, and her bridegroom, Carly. Such a nice couple. Everyone is saying that Don Vino is not really losing a daughter. No, actually, in this kind of Family, he'll probably lose a Son-in-law.

And so, with such a strange family and such weird children

THE ODD

This is some swell wedding!

It's THE Social event of 1945!

Everybody who is anybody in organized crime is here!

Look! Here comes the Odd Father!

They say he's the biggest Mafia leader in the country!

Hey, you! I'm with the Italian Anti-Defamation League! Don't you know you're not supposed to use the word "MAFIA" in this picture!?!

Sorry! Er—they say he's the biggest Italian racketeer and murderer in the country!

That's much better!

This is Sinny Minestrone, the Don's eldest son. He's next in line, and it's only a matter of time before he gets the Family business. That is, of course, unless a rival Family decides to give him the business first.

This is the Don's second son, Freako. He's a sad, gentle soul. He cries at weddings and all kinds of Family crises. But he can also be a barrel of laughs. Just catch him at a funeral some time.

This is Tim Haven, the Don's adopted son. He's shrewd and smart. All his life, he dreamed of being a criminal lawyer. But he only finished half of his education —the "criminal" part.

And this is Micrin, the Don's youngest son. He's a college graduate, a veteran war hero, an honest law-abiding citizen —and a disgrace to the entire Family.

It's easy to see why Don Vino Minestrone is known as...

FATHER

ARTIST: MORT DRUCKER
WRITER: LARRY SIEGEL

What a fantastic **make-up** job they've done on **Marlin Brandow**! How did they ever get him to look so **OLD**?

Very simple! They made him watch his **last four movies**, and he aged 20 years!

I still can't believe it's Marlin Brandow!

Mumble mumble mumble mumble

It's Marlin Brandow, all right!!

...IT IS YOUR HONOR TO INVITE ME TO YOUR DAUGHTER'S BRISS...

Papa, I'm so happy on my Wedding Day! Why aren't you happy too? Why do you look so pained?!?

You think it's **easy** to see your little girl grow up? You think it's **easy** to give her away to another man? You think it's **easy** to talk with **eight pounds of cotton** in your cheeks?

But **you** talk like that **WITHOUT** cotton in your cheeks!

5

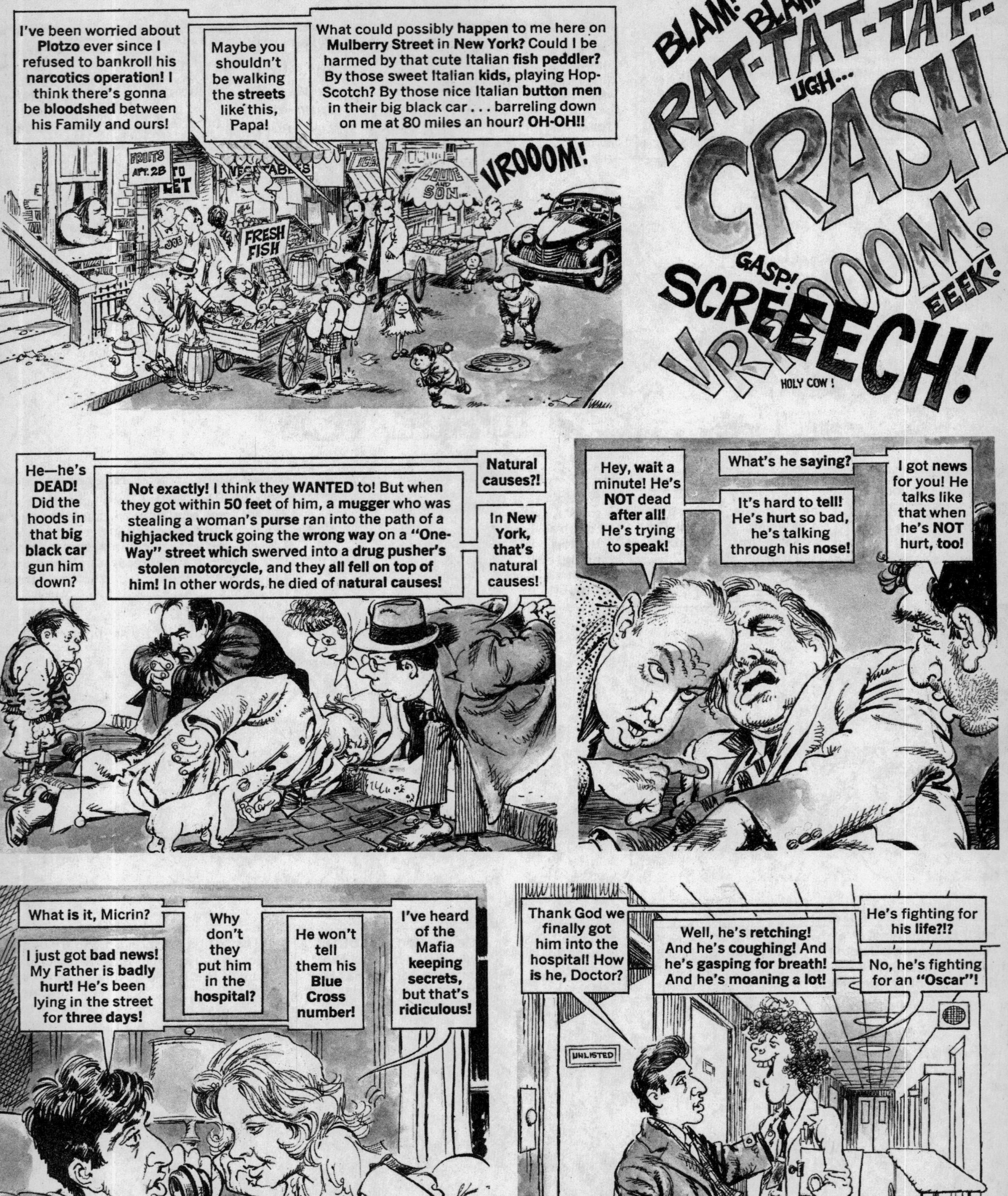

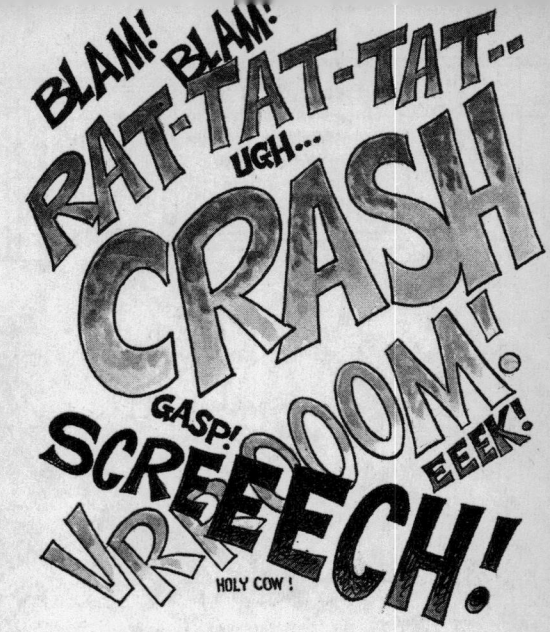

Whew! I almost blew it! Oh, boy, am I scared! Now, where's that gun? Where did they stash it? Maybe they left a message telling me where it's hidden? Oh, here's something written on the wall! It says, "Here I sit, broken-hearted..." No, that's not it!

Got it!! Okay, now all I gotta do is remember what they taught me... Walk out calmly... go up to Plotzo... shoot him twice in the face... drop the gun... and leave! That's simple enough! Be calm... be cool... and above all, DON'T PANIC!!

SHRIEK!! AAAAHH! SHREIK!! SCREEEAMM!

TAKE THAT, PLOTZO, YOU &¢%$*#!

BLAM!

What happened? Some maniac came out of the Men's Room firing a gun!

Looks like he shot everybody in the place! Everybody but HIM!!

How did HE get it? From complications brought on by eating too much scungilli, veal parmigiana and lasagna! In other words... he died of natural causes!

Natural causes?! In an Italian restaurant, that's natural causes!

It's great to have you home again, Papa! And I got good news for you! Micrin took care of Plotzo!

My little boy's first killing! I'm so proud of him! Remind me to have his gun bronzed!

Where is he now... in Sicily... waiting for the heat to die down?

No, in the bathroom, waiting for his stomach to die down!

You rotten &¢%$! How can you serve me this lousy &¢%$#@! You know I wanted chicken tetrazzini, pepperoni, ravioli, vermicelli, manicotti and zabaglione!

I know!! ...But for breakfast?!

What's that, Canny?!? Carly beat you up again! That dirty &¢%$#! I'll kill him! Hold him till I get there! What? I don't know HOW! Hit him over the head or tie him up or something!

Wait! I got a better idea! Serve him a seven course Italian meal! He won't be able to move for five hours!

10

Mort Drucker ON CARICATURE
by nick meglin

"There's more to caricature than drawing a humorous portrait. The resemblance is achieved by capturing the features, but it's the subtle nuances of a person—little highly individual touches—that breathe life into the work. I don't believe a caricature begins and ends with a face: figure, stance, attitude, expression—all add up to recognition. We can tell our friends or family members from strangers even when we can't see the face, and you can often spot someone you know by his walk. I have a special interest in hands. They tell a whole story in themselves. By matching the expression of the face with the correct hand gesture you can give the work more meaning, dimension, and humor than you can by just capturing a good likeness."

Drucker is not of the "lollipop" school of caricature, which consists of drawing the head and sticking it on a body—any body! A "lollipopist's" oeuvre will reveal that the figures are interchangeable. Some attempts may be made to broaden the girth of a heavy personality or stretch the frame of a tall one, but the effort ends after these cliché elements are incorporated.

From the beginning, Drucker considers the *total* person rather than the isolated parts. The personality starts to emerge even in his first quick, rough pencil notations. Though mere ovals serve as heads in this early stage we can, for example, distinguish a Jason Robards, Jr., from a George C. Scott. For even here, Drucker's astounding feel for the individual shows through: despite the crudity of the preparatory sketches, suggestions of Robard's long, narrow face are evident, as compared to Scott's broad forehead and Romanesque features.

The face

While the varied physical properties of an individual help establish total caricature, one's face remains the prime recognition factor. We are, of course, an eye-to-eye communicative society, responding to vocal stimuli by direct confrontation. The same holds true of the printed page. We "read" the face as we read the words.

For this reason, exaggeration for exaggeration's sake is not the way to accurate caricature. A dedicated caricaturist does more than draw big noses. He *reconstructs* the head to make all his exaggerations work together, placing in sharpest focus those features he believes best capture the personality.

"We all have the same features," states Drucker. "It's the space between them, their proportions and relationships to each other that distinguish one face from another. I let features swim around the facial area until I feel they've been arranged properly and the spacial relationships are right."

(continued on page 49)

"FAMILY" REUNION DEPT.

When last we saw the beloved Minestrone Family three years (and a couple of hundred bodies, and several Academy Awards, and $100 million in box office grosses) ago, God had made Vino, the original Odd Father, an offer he couldn't refuse and called him to that "Great Pizzeria In The Sky," and Micrin, Vino's youngest son, had taken over. We pick up the action again with Micrin Minestrone as Head of the Family and determined to prove that *he* can play...

THE O PA

ODD FATHER RT, TOO!

This **Communion** is wrecking my **schedule**, so I'll have to combine business with pleasure! Now, did you **blow up** those **three Las Vegas hotels** like I told you, Tim?

Yes, it's been **taken care of!**

Good! Well, so much for **pleasure!** Now to **business!** What happened to the **Boy's Choir** . . . ?

Vinny rubbed them out!

My God! Give me **one good reason** why!

When somebody said the **Choir** was going to **sing** . . . Vinny thought it was to the **COPS!**

That's a good reason!

Micrin, all these people are waiting to kiss the **Odd Father's** hand and ask you for your **council**—or for a **favor!**

We go in **order of importance** —the **biggest crooks first!**

Sal Valducci! I'm in charge of **narcotics** in New York!

Sorry! Not big enough!

I'm **Frankie Jamminjelli** —a **Detroit Don!** I just had **46 men** wiped out!

Listen, everybody! I said the **BIGGEST CROOKS FIRST!!** Who are you . . . ?

I'm a **United States Senator!**

Now we're talking! **YOU'RE FIRST!**

ARTIST: MORT DRUCKER   WRITER: LARRY SIEGEL

Mr. **Minestrone**, on your plan to take over all of Las Vegas, I've got **news** for you!

Kiss my hand and speak . . .

I want **$250,000** . . . and a **piece of the action!**

Kiss my **ass** and **leave!**

I must see **Micrin!**

You'll have to wait in line like the **rest of us,** Lady!

I can't believe it! I'm Number **62** in line, and I'm his **SISTER!**

What are **YOU** complaining about?!? I'm Number **74**, and I'm his **WIFE!**

Micrin . . . this is my **boy friend, Moil!** I'd like to marry him!

Him?!? This **creep?!** He's no **Husband** for an **Italian girl!** He's **not** one of **OUR KIND!**

But he **loves** me! He's tender and gentle . . . and he never hits me!

See? I **TOLD** you he's not one of our kind!

15

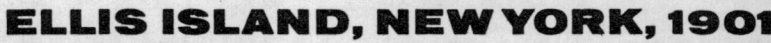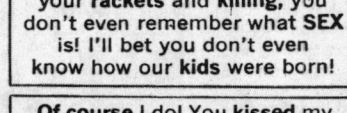

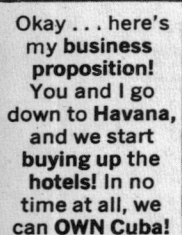

LAKE TAHOE, 1959

Well, there goes Freako! And there goes the hotel deal!

Hey, everybody! I think this is turning into a Surprise Party!

Oh, yeah? What's the surprise? SURPRISE!!

And there goes the country!

It's great being home, Tim! But I missed being here for the Holidays! So give me a run-down! What did you get my Son, Antonio, as a Christmas present from me?

Detroit!

Kids nowadays are spoiled rotten! When I was a kid, the most my Father ever got me was Staten Island!

WASHINGTON, D.C. 1959

Micrin, things are piling up! You got scores to settle with Herman Roth and Freako... and now a Senate Investigating Committee wants you to appear before them in Washington!

A Senate Committee? Uh-oh!! That could mean the end of our whole operation! By the way, who owns Washington?

Your daughter, Maria! You got it for her last Christmas!

I think we got a fighting chance!

Mr. Minestrone, you have been called before this Senate Committee because we are determined to wipe out the cancer that is threatening to destroy America in the '50's! State your name and line of work... and no lying!

I am Micrin Minestrone! I am the Capo of Capos in the Mafia! I control all prostitution, gambling and narcotics in this country! I deal in extortion, blackmail and murder! And I won't stop until the whole world is mine!

Mr. Minestrone, stop stalling! Are you now, or have you ever been a Communist?

No... I swear it!

Thank you, and God bless you!

NEW YORK CITY, 1917

What is the meaning of today's Religious Festival, Papa?

We are grateful that we Italians have lived through the past year, and we are asking the Almighty to please let us all live through the coming year!

And do you think that the Almighty... Don Tuttifrutti... WILL let us all live through the coming year, Papa?

Yes, if we give him a little respect, a little devotion, and a lot of payola!

Bless you, Don Tuttifrutti... forever and ever... Amen!

Hail, Don Tuttifrutti, our Beloved Savior!

Hey! How come Vino Minestrone is the only one around here who doesn't respect me? How come he doesn't offer prayers to me like the others?

But I heard him offer you a prayer a while ago!

Yeah? Well, you tell him that, "Don Tuttifrutti, you're some cutie!" is just not good enough!

19

SON OF THE SUMMER OF '42 DEPT.

A couple of years ago, there was a big wave of nostalgia. And you know what happens when you get caught up in a wave. After a while, it makes you nauseous. Which is what happened to us when we

THE CLO

Hi! Remember us? **Wormy**, **Husky** and **Beanie**, the "fun kids" from **"The Summer of '42"**? Maybe you don't remember how incredibly **cute** we were, or how incredibly **adorable** we were...

But you could **never** forget how incredibly **DULL** we were! Well, it's **two years later** ... and we're about to graduate High School on our way to becoming incredibly dull **adults!**

And we're not **shy, hung-up kids** anymore! We're **different!** Even **Husky**, here, has been **sexually liberated!** In fact, he's **SO** sexually liberated, he tries to make out with **everyone!**

See what I mean!?

You come here often? You need a lift home, Baby?

You can't even do **THAT** right! You're supposed to blow in my **ear**, not my **nose!**

ARTIST: MORT DRUCKER

Gee, Husky... I wish you'd try to make out with **smarter** girls!!

Why's that, Wormy...?

'Cause when you blow in **THIS** one's ear, the air comes right through!

saw "The Summer of '42"! Recently, not content to leave bad enough alone, the Producers of that sickening movie decided to try again! Well, they tried, all right! Mainly our patience, with...

DS OF '44

In that first picture, I made out...

But in this picture, I make out!

Hey, how about ME?!? When do I make out?!?

You come here often? You need a lift home, Baby?

I mean with GIRLS!!

...and as I look out across this sea of young, eager faces, I feel a little sad! Because, while some of you are headed for College, and others are headed for Military Service, I know that there is one fate that you are ALL headed for...

...a terrible case of acne!

WRITER: STAN HART

G'night, Wormy! Hey... I'm gonna make out with this one tonight for sure!

How do you know?

'Cause she'll do anything I want! I figure all I've gotta do is be nice to her and buy her a soda!

When does she get the soda... before or after?

DURING!! That way, she'll be too busy to notice what I'm doing!

So, Husky? How'd you make out!

Everything BUT...

Everything but WHAT?

I dunno! I'm still new at it!

Wow! Do you see what I see! I could jump all over that and let my hands go crazy and feel and squeeze...

Big deal! Let's see you do it!

Okay! I will!

31

YANGTZE, GO HOME! DEPT.

Since we live in such a peaceful world with no wars or violence, Hollywood moviemakers are finding it difficult to come up with subjects for War Movies. So they've got to dig into the past. This recent epic film was suggested by an actual incident that amazed the world... not because of what happened, but because it was forgotten so fast. And it certainly wasn't worth being reminded about it either, judging from

THE "SAM PEBBLES"

ARTIST: MORT DRUCKER   WRITER: STAN HART

Hi! I'm Jake Holenhead! There's only one thing I really love, and that's steam engines!

What are you doing stuck out here in China?

I once got a steam engine into trouble!

I'm Shrilly DuGood, and I'm going to teach Chinese children in our Mission School!

Gee, a girl like you shouldn't be talking to a sailor like me!

Oh, that's so prudish! Why shouldn't I talk to you?

Because you bore me to death!

Besides, you talk funny!

I'm not really talking! My ventriloquist father, Edgar Beggen, is working me!

You know, his lips move more than yours!

I think it's terrible—stationing our troops here in China, trying to foster a Political Philosophy that is completely alien to these simple people!

Missionary work!

Really, Reverend? And what are YOU doing here in China?

I see! Trying to foster a Religious Philosophy that is completely alien to these simple people!

Is this the "U.S.S. Sam Pebbles"?

No, it's the sightseeing cruise around Manhattan, and we're docked in Chinatown!

My name is Holenhead!

Oh? Are you French?

The boys call me "Frenchy"!

No, I was born in Brooklyn!

37

Brooklyn?! Then why do you have a British accent?
My folks gave it to me for my Bar Mitzvah!
Well, I still don't know why the boys call you "Frenchy"!
Because it sounds so "loveable"!
That's too bad!
What's too bad?
Don't you ever go to the movies? Don't you know what always happens to loveable guys in "War Pictures"?
Always??
ALWAYS!!
I'm Captain of this ship, and I live for only one thing—that flag up there! I'll protect it! I'll defend it! I'll die for it!
You really love your country, eh, Captain?
No, I just have this "thing" about Silk! Don't you?
I'm a "Suede Man" myself, Sir!
Now, remember—on my ship, the coolies do all the work!
Don't the coolies object?
Shh! They think they're learning "Democracy"
See that new "Bar-Girl", Jack? I've just fallen in love with her!
Why her, Frenchy?
Because she's so loveable!
That's too bad!
You mean—?
You know the bit, Frenchy! Loveables . . . in a "War Movie"!
Gee, why couldn't I fall in love with a rotten girl!?
How'dy'do, Ma'am! My buddy is dying to meet you! This is "Frenchy"!
My name is "Dingaling," and I can buy my freedom for $200!
Why $200?
That is a long story! Nobody knows it but me!
And you won't tell it to anyone?
I tell it to everyone! But nobody ever stays awake to the end! I said it was a long story!
You're crazy, Holenhead! You can't teach those dumb coolies anything!
You'll see! I'll make this guy into a first class engine room man!
Hoo-hah! I gonna be flirst crass engine loom man!

Panel 1:
- This is a boiler!
- Boi-rah!
- Boil-er!
- Boi-ruh!

Panel 2:
- This is a drive shaft!
- Duhlive shaff!
- Dr-rive shaft!
- Dlive shaff!

Panel 3:
- Okay, show these creeps what you've learned!
- The rain in Spain falls mainly in the plain!
- By George, he's got it!

Panel 4:
- This is a pressure valve!
- Plessure vawuv!
- Pr-ressure val-ve!
- Pl-lessure vaw-wuv!

Panel 5:
- This is a propellor!
- Forget it, Jake!

Panel 6:
- All right, men— what am I bid for this lovely little Oriental beauty...?
- Oh, Frenchy— please save me!
- Who's gonna bid a dollar? Seventy-five cents? Half a buck? We'll throw in a set of steak knives and a dozen hand towels! A quarter?

Panel 7:
- C'mon, Dingaling! While the free-for-all-fight we started is going on, I'll get you out of here!
- Wouldn't it have been easier to just bid a quarter? Then you'd own me!
- Own you for a quarter?! What a terrible thing to say! Do you think quarters grow on trees?

Panel 8:
- ...and I take you, Dingaling, for my wife!
- Do you think they'll be happy?
- I doubt it! They're not really married!
- Because they don't have a Clergyman?
- No, because they don't have a Caterer! A wedding isn't official until the Bride feeds the Groom a hot hors d'oeuvre!

Panel 9:
- They look so happy! We ought to get married too, Jack!
- Do you think the three of us could be happy?
- The three of us?
- You, me, and your father!
- You mean the FIVE of us!! Don't forget my brothers— Charlie McCarthy and Mortimer Snerd!

39

Panel 1:
- We're surrounded by Nationalist Chinese junks! They won't let us out of the harbor! We'll miss the last tide before Winter!
- Let's blast our way out!
- That's what they want us to do! Imagine what propaganda that would make! No, I won't give them the satisfaction!
- Then what are we going to do?
- Stay right here and starve all Winter! That'll be one on them!

Panel 2:
- We've been trapped on board all Winter! I've got to see Dingaling! Don't try to stop me, Jake! I warn you, don't try! There's no use trying to stop me!
- I'm not trying to stop you, Frenchy!
- Some pal you are! I could freeze to death in the icy water!

Panel 3:
- I'm so glad you came, Jack! Frenchy caught pneumonia, and I gave him an old Chinese remedy to see what would happen!
- And what did you find out?
- I found out why you don't see too many OLD Chinese around! It didn't work!

Panel 4:
- Captain, they want Holenhead! They say he killed Frenchy and Dingaling!
- You'd better turn Holenhead over to them or they'll kill us all!
- Boy, talk about self-centered buddies! What ever happened to the great sailor of yesteryear and the "one-for-all-and all-for-one" tradition of Dick Powell and James Cagney and Pat O'Brien?

(Signs: GIVE US HORENHEAD / GET OUT of VIETNAM)

Panel 5:
- Give him up, Captain!
- Or else we'll take over the ship!
- Men, there hasn't been a mutiny on a United States warship since the "USS Herman Wouk"! If you go through with this, I'll show you something you'll never forget... a Captain, crying!

Panel 6:
- Besides, we've got a job to do upriver! The Chinese are threatening the American Mission, and we've got to rescue the Reverend and that dummy schoolteacher!
- But we're not supposed to get involved in this revolution! That would be against orders, Captain!
- Orders are not official until they're recorded in the logbook! What does it say in the logbook?
- Port is left... Starboard is right!
- Not that page, you idiot!

40

Look, Captain— a line of junks . . . blocking the river!
Looks like we'll **have** to get involved! Now, remember, men, these Chinese are defending their homeland, their rights, and their hopes of finding a better way of life!
What should we **do?**
Fight dirty!
We're fighting to **free** our country of **exploiters** and **foreign marauders!**
I know! I'm **really** rooting for **your side!**
Someday, we will make our country **strong** so we can live in **peace** and **dignity!**
Gee, I sure **hope** so!
We've come to **rescue** you!
We're **not going!** The Chinese are our **friends!**
Actually, **ONE** Chinese is our friend! But since they **look alike,** he thinks **ALL Chinese** are our friends!
BLAM! BLAM
Well, he's been **shot** by his **Chinese "friends"! Now,** maybe he'll act a little **differently!**
That's for sure! **He's dead!**
I hope the Chinese will **throw off the yoke of Dictatorship,** someday, Captain!
Yes, Holenhead! Then they will be **free** to **choose** their **own leaders** and march happily toward **Democracy!**
BLAM! BLAM BLAM BLAM
Who shot **them?**
We did! Maybe we don't agree on **most** things, but . . .
. . . we **do** agree we **don't want** anyone talking about **Democracy** here in **China!**
MORT DRUCK

THE FRAT'S IN THE FIRE DEPT.

In the old days, kids would look up to "Groups"...like the New York Yankees or the Green Bay Packers... strong, skilled athletes who would set shining examples for the Youth of America to emulate. Later generations would idolize "Rock" Groups... like the Beatles or the Rolling Stones... funny-looking guys, yes, but at least they could sing. Today's kids are looking up to and emulating an entirely different kind of Group. This Group barfs, spits up, guzzles beer, molests women, flunks tests and holds orgies. Evidently, America's Youth feels this is lots more fun than playing ball or singing. We mean the Group from...

Er—Hi, guys! I'm **Dirk Neitchemeyer** ... Rush Chairman of Omooga House!

I'm **Leery Krocker**.

I'm **Kink Barfman**.

You guys are in the **wrong place!** The "Laurel and Hardy Look-Alike Contest" is downtown!

Uh— we're here to pledge your frat!

Are you kidding?!? We're clean-cut, blonde, blue-eyed "A" students and campus leaders! You're two slobs! Who'd believe it?!

That we came to rush your frat?

No! That in **this** movie, **WE** turn out to be the **"BAD GUYS,"** and **YOU'RE** gonna be the **"GOOD GUYS"**!!

As **President** of this, the most **conservative**, **classiest** fraternity on campus, I'm sorry to say you two clowns don't fit our image!

What **IS** our image?!

Let me put it this way: If **Hitler** had known how to **play tennis**, we would've **pledged** him immediately!

ABOMINAL HOUSE

Look at those two! A **wimp** and a **blimp!**

Can you **imagine** those two wanting to join a **frat** house?

Yeah! The **fat** guy **IS** a frat house!

Let's go! I don't think we're **wanted** here!

What do you mean, **"WE"**, Tubbo!

DOLTA HOUSE...! Now, **THIS** frat house is **better** for us! Already, I have that **warm** feeling all over!

Hi, I'm **Pluto**, the most **disgusting student** on campus! I'm **also** one of the **funniest men** you'll see on film this year!

He **IS** funny! I'm laughing so hard, the **tears** are rolling down my **legs!**

Those aren't **tears**, jerk! I think he just **used** us as a **HYDRANT!!**

ARTIST: MORT DRUCKER   WRITER: ARNIE KOGEN   ADDITIONAL DIALOGUE: DICK DE BARTOLO

Welcome to **Dolta House** ... the **freakiest frat house** on campus! Help yourselves to the **refreshments!** We've got cookies, punch, pizza, soda, pickles, beer and ice cream!

What's so **freaky** about that??

All mixed together in one **huge** bowl?!?

How come they're all dressed up inside the house?

'Cause we're **Doltas**, and we **don't** do anything **normal** here! You've heard of **"Strip Poker"?** They're playing **"DRESS Poker"!**

Hey! Who's that?

What's he doing?

I mean **WHY** is he riding his **motorcycle** up the stairs?

Oh, that's **V-J** Day!

About **35 miles** an **hour!!**

Because if he rode his **BUICK** up, he'd probably **scrape hell** out of the **bannister!**

43

Listen, guys . . . we just can't keep on rejecting pledgees by throwing things at the movie screen!
No . . . we're running out of movie screens!
Why? Are we running out of pledgees . . . ?
Now this next guy is Leery Krocker! Any comments . . . ?
The kid's okay!
Yeah!
Alright! Krocker is in! How about this next pledgee?
AAAAAGHHHHH!
No! Not him! I don't want HIM here!
Not NOW! Not while I'm running away with this picture! I don't need him around to start stealing scenes!
You are now officially Doltas! Your Dolta name is "Pin Head"!
How come it's "Pin Head"?
Because in this family magazine, we can't call you "$@#%¢&-Head"!
Gee, it's gonna be fun being a fraternity guy in 1962! "Pep Rallies"—"Panty Raids"—"Phone Booth-Stuffing"!
Forget "Phone Booth-Stuffing"! We'd both need our own booth!
That's right! We ARE both "fatties"!
Look at the bright side! The way YOUR body looks, and MY body looks, let's be glad "Streaking" isn't popular yet!!
PHHT
LOUIE . . . LOUIE . . . WHOA . . . NO . . . BABY . . . BABY . . . WE GOTTA GO . . . BOMP . . . BOMP . . . YA-YA-YA-YA-YA!
It's amazing!
That they all sing so bad?
No, that the "Sound Track Album" is doing as well as the movie!
Grogg . . . what's the worst fraternity on campus?
Gee, that's hard to say, Dean Wormy!
Cut the B. S., Grogg! It's the DOLTA house! I've got their disciplinary file right here! Listen:
Back in 1956, they threw a "Surprise Pajama Party" and held 34 Co-eds captive for 10 days in their basement!
In '58, they kidnapped 11 Co-eds, poured pancake syrup over their bodies and tried to pass them off as Farber's first Negro Sorority!
The next year, they stole the Cheerleaders' bras, cut them in half, and sold them as "yamulkas" to B'nai Brith!
And last year, they got hold of 5 corpses, sat them at tables at the Alumni Dinner . . .
And for the entire evening, nobody noticed the difference between the corpses and the living guests!
Gee, Sir, what do you want me to do?
I want you to get me INTO that FRAT!
DEAN WORMY
LOVE THY NEIGHBOR
LOVE THY ENEMY
LOVE LAURIE BACHNER
DOLTA HOUSE

But—you can't join a Frat, Dean Wormy!
Then as of this moment, I'm putting them on DOUBLE SECRET PROBATION!
Double Secret Probation?!? What's that?
How should I know?! That's part of the secret! !
I hate those creeps at Dolta! I have the feeling that even now one of 'em is pulling some underhanded trick . . .
Close, Dean Wormy . . .! Close . . .
I've locked the doors and pulled the shades because I thought you might want to join me in an "avant-garde", really mind-blowing experience for 1962 . . . a real head-trip!
Gee! Are we going to smoke POT?!
Don't be a fool! Pot will be around for years! We're gonna listen to a MORT SAHL album!
Let's see . . . we owe you $10.50, Pluto . . .
WHAT?! He ate $23.00 worth of food on line, he's got $16.00 worth on his plate . . . and YOU'RE paying HIM?!?
That's our deal! Since he's been on campus, we haven't paid one cent for Clean-up or Sanitation! Pluto, here, eats all the garbage!
Not ALL the garbage! I didn't eat the script for this movie!
Hey . . . guess what I am . . .!
What's the slob up to now?!?
I'm not sure, but you better not ask him to pass those mashed potatoes . . .!
I'm a ZIT! Get it?
That boy is an absolute PIG!
Disgusting!
You're lucky! Next, he does his impression of a "festering sore", using a fried banana!
FOOD FI-I-IGHT! !
A food fight! ! What a healthy outpouring of uninhibited fun!
Now, this embodies the true spirit of Higher Education in America!
Y'know, this "Cafeteria Scene" has really caught on with the kids! It's become a cult favorite!
Yeah! Kids all over the country are parking in Lovers Lanes and spitting potatoes at each other!
How unfair, and totally inconsiderate!
What a terrible, terrible waste!
Don't they know there are starving comedians in India . . . just DYING to use food as props!?!
God . . . I hate corn!
That's not corn, lady! That's CREAMED SPINACH!
Idiot! I'm not talking about what we're THROWING! I'm talking about what we're DOING!

I've come to this hell-hole of a fraternity to set you creeps straight! You clowns are the scum of the campus! Your house grade-point average is a disgrace, the lowest in Farber history! And your behavior. . . your drinking and carousing could get you expelled! Now, what do you plan to do about it?
We plan to throw a "Toga Party". . . raise hell. . . and seduce your wife!
Good! As long as we understand each other!
CIRCUS
KEEP OUT
Tell me, what exactly IS a "Toga Party" anyway?
It gives us a chance to put on sheets and go berserk!
Y'know, there's another bunch of guys into that!
Another frat . . . here on campus?
No, the Ku Klux Klan!
Right But I don't think they'd hire the same band!
SHOUT—A LITTLE BIT SOFTER NOW! SHOUT—A LITTLE BIT LOUDER NOW! SHOUT—A LITTLE BIT REPETITIOUS NOW! SHOUT—A LITTLE BIT BORING NOW! SHOUT—IT'S SO NOISY NOW!
CAESARS
Are you wearing anything under that sheet?
Would you like to see? ?
No, thanks! I wouldn't want to spoil this swell time I'm having.
Well, I think Pluto looks simply adorable!
It wasn't easy! He had to go to every Men's Shop in town to find a size 48 stout Contour Sheet!
Where do you guys get that unbridled energy?! All these orgies. . . all these zany pranks . . . going crazy-wild every Saturday night . . .!!
That's just for kicks . . . for now, while we're in college! When we grow up and become respectable citizens, I don't think we'll be making our livings by going crazy-wild every Saturday night!
Hey . . .speak for yourself, chum
Hi, Punto . . .!
Hey! Why, it's Chlorine, the girl I picked up in the Supermarket! I'm glad you could make it!
I got some catching up to do! What do you have to drink?
Man, she's a boozer! I've got it MADE!!
How about some 12-year-old Bourbon?!?
No, thank you! I make it a rule never to drink anything OLDER than I am!
Whoops!
Well! Dean Wormy's wife! Welcome . . .! You're just what this party needs! . . . Another drunk!
The Dean is very upset, Udder! He found out that you were cheating!
On my Midterm Exams?!?
No . . . With ME!
But . . . I haven't cheated with you!
Let's go upstairs to the bedroom . . . and talk about it!

Panel 1:
- I'm—I'm sorry about all this TISSUE PAPER, Leery...
- Oh, I understand! You have to pack those things very carefully so they don't break while you're dancing!

Panel 2:
- The meeting of the Pan-Hellraising Disciplinary Committee will come to order! Proceed directly with the charges against— yech — Dolta House!
- It is charged that Dolta House members are guilty of the following disgusting, perverted and obscene acts!
- 1. Conducting a lewd Toga Party! 2. Having intimate relations with a minor! 3. Having intimate relations with a chicken!
- 4. Roller skating on a virgin! 5. Dancing the twist on the Mayor's face!
- 6. Opening an umbrella inside a campus Policeman's pants! 7. Finger-painting a Pom-Pom Girl!
- Hey... no one's perfect! So I painted outside the lines!!

Panel 3:
- This whole trial is a farce!!
- It's a ream job!
- Shut up, you clowns! And sit down!
- You can't do anything to us! We have a little more POWER than you!!
- Are you kidding?! I'm the DEAN of this college!!
- Yeah, but some of US are the writers of this picture!!
- NUTS!

Panel 4:
- Well, I guess he DID have more power than us! He took away our charter, expelled us from Farber, and gets all our future first-born children... that belong to his wife!
- What are we gonna do now? We gotta get even!!
- We could mess up their big Homecoming Day Parade!
- Great idea! We'll enter a FLOAT!
- Where we gonna get a float?
- We have one right here... PLUTO!
- No good! We need something we can MOVE!

Panel 5:
- May I have 288 marbles, please!
- That's two gross!
- NOTHING's too gross for this movie!

Panel 6:
- Okay, men... let's circumcise our watches!
- You mean... "SYNCHRONIZE our watches," don't you?!?
- No... I mean "CIRCUMCISE"! We've got an "R" rating to uphold!

Panel 7:
- It's a perfect day for the parade, Mayor DePatsy! The air is crisp, the floats are gay and colorful, the girls are young and pretty... Nothing could possibly go wrong!
- You really think so, Dean Wormy?
- I sure do! Oh, by the way... I was also a LOOKOUT at PEARL HARBOR!

Dean Wormy, look!! Where did that ridiculous CAKE float come from?!
Oh, it was probably entered by one of our GAY frats—OH! NO!
It's those clowns from DOLTA HOUSE! They're trying to destroy our parade . . .!!
MOXIE'S
DTX
And I think they're SUCCEEDING!!
Just look at those college kids . . . smoking pot, driving recklessly, having no respect for anything! What can that possible train them for?
A career in Government Service!
DEATHMOBILE
You're FINISHED in this town, Wormy! You're FIRED!!
I quit, anyway!! College life here at Farber in 1962 is TOO TERRIFYING! I'm gonna spend the rest of the '60's teaching in a college where it will be PEACEFUL and QUIET!
Really . . .?!? Where are we moving to?
A Place called BERKELEY.
Does this movie have a message?
Yeah . . . that television isn't as bad as we thought.
What do we do now, Pluto?
We end the picture!
But there IS no end to this picture!
Then we cop the same ending that "American Graffiti" used when THEY had no end to THEIR picture!
You mean . . .?!?
You got it . . .!! "Where Are They Now?" photos!! Roll 'em!!
VINCENT JAMES DAY '63
Legal Assistant to Ralph Nader.
ROBERT HOOVERVAC '63
Had Sex-Change Operation. Now A Leading Female Tennis Pro.
KINK BARFMAN '66
Missing Since 1971. Rumored To Have Been Sucked Into A Tuba.
G. BRENT MARMALADE '63
Rabbi—Temple B'nai Loaded Rockville Centre, New York.
DIRK NEITCHEMEYER '63
Successful Stand-up Comedian Hollywood, California.
DEAN VERNAL WORMY '48
Burned At Stake During Student Demonstations, Berkeley, 1967.
MRS. WORMY 38-27-38
Arrested For Molesting A Minor Now Serving 10-20, Chattahoochee.
JOHN MOP PLUTO '63
Advisor to Pres. Nixon '68-'72
Advisor to Pres. Ford '73-'74
Advisor to Pres. Carter '74—

Photographs: aid, not answer

Drucker doesn't copy or trace photographs, but he often uses them for research, as a basis for his work. They also serve to remind him of what he has personally observed from movies or television. A keen observer, he retains many visual responses. Drucker studies the expressions and nuances of a person much as Rich Little, Frank Gorshin, or other impersonators would, basing their mimicry on a level deeper than mere speech imitation. Drucker gets to the heart of the character and works diligently to maintain his graphic likeness.

The vision of the artist can in some ways be truer than that of the photograph. This brings to mind Picasso's retort when criticized that his portrait of Gertrude Stein didn't look like the famed writer: "Never mind," the artist said, "in the end *she* will look like the *portrait!*" Picasso's explanation was more than playful. He knew he'd captured his subject as he knew her through their friendship. Subsequently, Miss Stein did indeed "grow" into the resemblance. The portrait, painted about the turn of the century, is perhaps the most definitive study of Gertrude Stein ever executed.

Learned by doing

"I'm extremely fortunate," states Drucker, "in that everything I know about caricature I learned through professional experience. There were no months of study or books to study from—and even if there had been, there was no time for it. The assignment was there, calling for humorous rather than "straight" likenesses, and I had to deliver as any other professional artist would. After the job was accepted and paid for, I said 'Hey! I can do caricatures!' And that was that. I didn't realize at any time it would turn out to be the most important facet of my work and career."

Like many others who specialize in continuity illustration (telling a story through a panel-by-panel technique as opposed to a single illustration), Drucker began his career in comic books. And, like so many others in this field, his dream at the time was to "graduate" from this notoriously ill-paying field to a syndicated daily and/or Sunday feature newspaper. While a syndicated strip doesn't guarantee financial independence, it at least allows those involved a royalty arrangement whereby their incomes increase concurrent with the popularity of their work. This concept, of course, serves as an incentive to keep work at the highest possible level. Comic books, on the other hand, paid by the page. With the exception of a few rare individuals, each artist was paid at the same page rate, depending upon the company. In this setup, *speed* rather than *quality* becomes the factor that decides income. Quality becomes a very relative term. A six-page story, for example, cannot be judged by the work alone, but by the level an artist can maintain while still trying to earn a living.

Comic books are enjoying a new wave of interest and high sales. However, as long as the "pay by the pound" policy prevails, quality work will be delivered by a talented few who have the ability to turn out good work at a rate of speed that still enables them to feed their families. Drucker worked under such conditions but found it very hard to derive much pleasure or satisfaction from his work. He marveled at a Joe Kubert, an Alexander Toth, or a Jack Davis, whose work, he felt, was the quintessence of comic book art.

(continued p. 63)

GRIT AND BEAR IT DEPT.

*My name is **Brattie Ross!** I am 14 years old, and I am the **heroine** of the movie you are about to see!*

*In addition to being rather **overbearing** and **long-winded** for someone my age... I also **talk funny!***

*I talk funny mainly because I do **not** use any **contractions!** Perhaps you do not know what a contraction **is!***

*A contraction is a convenient way to shorten a group of words, which—as you can see—I have not done in **six possible spots** in this clumsy speech that you are now reading...*

TRUE

Incidentally, this movie has a **"G" Rating,** which means that it is perfectly all right for **children** to see because it does not have any **sex** in it. What it **does** have in it, however, is plenty of **blood** and **gore** and **violence** and **killing**. According to those Hollywood self-censors, I guess **that** sort of stuff is **perfectly all right for children to see!** Like this scene in the beginning of the picture where my **father** gets shot to death by **Tom Shamey!**

BLAM! BLAM!

I am looking for **Tom Shamey** who killed my father! I shall need **money.** I believe you are holding **property** that **belonged** to my father! You shall pay me **$300** for it!

I'll pay you **$200** and not **one penny more!** And don't try to **bargain** with me! Only last week, I out-bargained the famous financier, **J. P. Morgan!**

Is J. P. Morgan as **shrewd** as me?

$300! Shrewder! $200!

50

| Oops! Make that **SEVEN** spots! | In this movie, I go through a series of **fantastic adventures!** At the end, I learn the meaning of **honor**, the meaning of **courage**, and the meaning of **life!** | Also, thanks to that great Western star, **John Weight**, I learn the meaning of... |

FAT

ARTIST: MORT DRUCKER **WRITER: LARRY SIEGEL**

"You'll **pay** for this crime, Tom Shamey! You'll never get **away** with it! You'll be **hounded** and **hunted** for the rest of your **life** until you're **caught** and **hanged** by the neck until dead!"

"By **who?** Wyatt Earp, the fastest gun in the West??"

"No... by my **daughter** Brattie... the fastest **TONGUE** in the West!"

"Oh, **Gawd!!** Anyone but **that** pushy little broad!!"

"Does he have as much **business savvy?**"
"$300!"
"Much more!"
"$200!"

"Can he hold his breath till his face turns blue??"

"Okay! OKAY!! $300! If there's one thing I can't stand... it's a blue-faced kid!"

She talked me out of four horses!
She talked me out of 14 guns and 300 rounds of ammunition!
She talked me out of two months supply of provisions!
What a daughter I got! That Brattie is some girl!
Hey, Ross . . . ain't you dead?!
I was— but she talked me out of it!
UNDERTAKER
You cain't violate the laws of God!! Lucky for you I'm a religious man!
BLAM! BLAM!
I shall need a room for the night!
Go away! Don't you see the sign?! No children or pets allowed!
Perhaps you have heard of me? Brattie Ross— the pushy, blue-faced breath-holding kid?
Come on in, Miss Ross, and bring your horses!
NO CHILDREN OR PETS
You'll have t' share a bed with this little old lady!
I would prefer to sleep alone!
Stop worryin'! With YOU buggin' her, she'll never live through the night!
Very well! I shall take the room! Now I must get a Law Officer to help me find Tom Shamey!
Excuse me, Marshal! As soon as you put this bum in jail, I should like to offer you a business proposition!
Hold it, girl! I'M the Marshal! He's the BUM!
YOU'RE the Marshal?! A . . . a terrible drunk like you?!
Whatta yuh mean, "terrible"?! I'm the BEST drunk in these parts!
JAIL
I am looking for the murderer of my father! I would like a man with true fat to help me find him! Fat men are jolly, and I trust a jolly man!
Don't look at me, Sister! I may have true fat . . . but I'm not jolly!
The job pays $100 in hard cash!
Ho-Ho-Ho! Merr-r-y Christmas! MERR-R-Y CHRISTMAS!

Panel 1:
- Well, Marshal, will you take the job?
- Okay, but **first** let me tell you what this country is **all about**. Tom Shamey is a **criminal**, and your father is a **victim**. Unfortunately, too many people nowadays **worry** about criminals and **forget** about victims. I say a **victim** has **rights**, too! Doesn't a victim have **rights**?

Panel 2:
- Of course! Every victim in this big, beautiful country of ours has **God-given** rights passed down by our forefathers!
- Right! Except that @&¢#!! Tom Shamey! When he becomes **MY** victim, he has **NO** rights! He has just **one** thing! A hole in his gut! And **THAT's** what this country is all about!

Panel 3:
- Wow! You are even **more** long-winded than I am!
- Hold it! I'm not finished yet! See that rat!?
- EEK!
- BLAM! BLAM!

Panel 4:
- That rat I just killed ain't **JUST** a rat! To me, it's a **symbol**! That rat symbolizes cruel, un-American violence! Which is why **I** killed it with a clean American bullet! Now—look at me! What do you see? A fat-drunken, one-eyed slob?... **WRONG!!**
- I'm not **JUST** a fat, drunken, one-eyed slob! I'm a **symbol**! I symbolize all fat, drunken, one-eyed slobs who are not going to let **dirty rats** take over this **great country of ours** and flouridate our whiskey and give us Commie eye transplants and...
- Hmmm! While I usually admire fat patriots—sometimes there is a lot to be said for skinny traitors!

Panel 5:
- I hear tell you're Brattie Ross! My name is LaBeefy! I'm after Tom Shamey, **too**! I'd like to join your party!
- I do not trust you! For one thing, you do not have True **Fat**!
- That's only because I'm still young! Anyway, I **AM** starting to get jowly!
- No! I am sorry! True **CHUBBY** is not the same as True **FAT**!

Panel 6:
- Listen, can I go with you or NOT?
- I shall think about it! What do you do for a living?
- I'm a Free Lance Clod!
- Oh, **very** well. Come on along! We can always use some comic relief!

Panel 7:
- Mr. LaBeefy, I would like you to meet—
- Why... why you're masked! And that white horse! What an honor it is to meet the Masked Rider of the Plains! You... you're the Lone—
- Hey, dummy! This ain't no mask! It's an eye-patch!

Panel 8:
- Boy, is **HE** ever stupid! What's he doing in this picture?
- Well, let me put it this way... Without **HIM**, who would sing the title song—**YOU**?!

53

Shamey and his gang are holed up in that cabin there! I think we should attack 'em!
Hold it! Little girls don't attack bad guys! You stay here!
Those kid tricks don't bother me!!
I am going with you! I will hold my breath! I will whine! I will throw a temper tantrum! I will eat rocks! I . . .
Good! I am ready!
In that case, I shall pull the one kid-trick which NO adult has a defense against— the maddening "Echo Trick"!
What's the maddening Echo Trick?
What's the maddening Echo trick?
Cut that out, Brattie!
Cut that out, Brattie!
Okay, you asked for it!
Okay, you asked for it!
OWWW!
OWWW!
You are giving me a terrible pain in the rear end!
On behalf of the movie audience, and everyone else who has come in contact with you so far, that makes us even!
Now THAT'S what I like to see! HEALTHY American sex! None of that sick NUDE love-making you see in Commie movies nowadays!
While we're staking out the cabin— mind if I sing an old prairie song?
Oh-oh say can you see
By the dawn's early light
What so proud-ly we hail
At the twilight's last gleaming—
Can't he just sing a NORMAL cowboy lament . . . like "Cool Water" or "Tumblin' Tumble-weeds"?!
I do not mind the song so much! It is just that I find it hard to sleep while standing at attention!
And now, for my next number—
You can't do it, Marshal— You just can't do it!
Why not?
Because NOBODY sings "The Gettysburg Address"!
It's YOU! Tom Shamey! So we meet at last!
Do not worry! I will give you the chance you never gave my father! I will turn you over to Marshal Booster Claghorn who will see that you face true American justice!
Don't shoot! Don't shoot!
Shoot! Shoot! PLEASE SHOOT!!
BLAM
Never disobey a grown-up . . . I always say!

Booster, I have just shot Tom Shamey, and—Say! What is going on?
Those four guys are the rest of Shamey's gang! I am about to put my reins in my mouth and ride at them, shooting with both hands! It's a real fun-sport, and almost as bloody as Pro Football . . .
Booster, please don't ride at those four men with your reins in your mouth! It's dangerous! It's foolhardy! It's—Aw, now see what you made me do! You've got me so upset, I'm using contractions!
Taste hot lead, you polecats!
Booster, you are—without a doubt, the ugliest cowboy who ever lived!
You're fat and you're sloppy . . .
And you're drunk . . .
And you're one-eyed . . .
SURPRISE! I'm also toothless!
The kid was right! It IS dangerous riding with reins in your mouth!
The casualities are as follows: Four dead bad guys and one wounded horse . . . mine! From carryin' my weight for so far and for so long, the poor critter got himself a hernia!
Booster, you have really proven yourself to me! Yes, there is no doubt about it! You have TRUE FAT!!
Thanks, kid!
By the way, what happened to LaBeefy?
He was killed!
Very sad! I see now that he had True Fat also! Too bad it was all in his head!
Well, this is where we part company, Sister! I'm going into town to get a truss for my horse, and then I'm headin' for he sunset! What about you? What about your future . . .?
Who knows?! What kind of a future is there for a cranky, pushy girl who never stops talking?
Stop worrying! You're gonna make someone a great wife someday!
So long, Sister!
FRANK ROSS BORN MARCH 2 1880 DIED MAY 21 1885
There he goes . . . Booster Claghorn, a Marshal of the Old West! He is fat and sloppy and drunk and one-eyed and toothless! And yet—he is wonderful! Yes, in spite of his flaws . . .
. . . there will be a place for him in the future of this great America!
SUPPORT OUR BOYS IN THE U.S. CAVALRY!
THE INDIANS —AMERICA'S RED MENACE!
IF THE SIOUX DON'T LIKE IT HERE, LET THEM GO BACK WHERE THEY CAME FROM!
REGISTER THE JAMES GANG —NOT GUNS!

MUCHO DE NIRO DEPT.

For as long as we can remember, the plot of a "Fight Picture" was usually very simple. An underprivileged kid starts in the gutter, and blasts his way to the top. Then, along comes the first major Fight Picture of the '80's, and what do we get: an underprivileged kid starts in the gutter, and blasts his way to the sewer! Boy, Hollywood has given us our fair share of "anti-heroes" in the past, but now make way for the "anti-anti-anti hero" affectionately known as the...

RAVI

Wow! This is the greatest fight of 1941!

Look at that! A **White** man and a **Black** man, together in the **same** ring, beatin' each other's brains out!

Yeah! Who said integration would never work!?

That Jerk LaMutha ain't HU-MAN! He's never been knocked off his feet!!

He's never BEEN off his feet —period!! He even SLEEPS standing up!!

Are you sure?!? Only horses sleep standing up!

Trust me! He once spent two weeks in my stable!

They promised me a crack at LaMutha, but first I gotta win a couple of real easy warm-up fights!

Yeah...? With who?

The Japs and the Nazis!

Kill the friggin' bum, Jerk! Hit the frig right in his friggin' mouth!!

ARTIST: MORT DRUCKER

I can't believe it, Shmoey! It —it's my first loss! I dropped the decision!!

Big deal! So you lost! You gotta act like a MAN! You gotta do what's expected of you!

I guess you're right! Okay! Now beat up the Referee and the two Judges and let's go!

What's wrong with Jerk these days, Shmoey?

Why? He's his usual self! Mean, rotten, foul-mouthed and disgusting!

Yeah?!? How come he won't let the Mob buy into him? Why won't he throw fights?

Okay!! Okay!! Gee... I never said he was PERFECT

A STREET IN THE BRONX N.Y.

56

NG BULLY

WRITER: LARRY SIEGEL

I've never heard such language in my entire life!!

"Friggin' " is dirty?! They use worse language than that on Saturday Morning TV Cartoons!

For MAD Magazine it's dirty! Remember the good old days when MAD used to use "#@☆©!★" instead of curse words! They've sure come a long way!!

Using "friggin' " instead of ☆@☆!@☆ is some long way! On a flight from New York to L.A., that's like a forced landing in Jersey City!!

Hey, Jerk!! Destroy the friggin' bum! Tear the friggin' crud apart!!

FRIGGIN'! FRIGGIN'! That's all I hear! Enough already with that vile, disgusting word!!

KILL the @#&+%$@+ bum! Knock his @#$%&! head off!! Hey, who are you?!

The Editor of MAD Magazine... just taking a little trip down Memory Lane!!

I'M THE CHAMP! I'M THE CHAMP!

"I COULDA BEEN A CONTENDER"

Of all the guys in The Bronx, I had to marry you! Look at you! You ain't a man! You're an animal!!

An animal?! Hey, you friggin' broad! Don' ever call me an animal again! I may be just a pug, but I got pride and dignity! I ain't no animal!!

Okay! Okay! Now... how do you want your meat...? Raw, as usual?!?

Yeah! With maybe a li'l Gravy Train on the side!

Okay, here's your meat, Meat Head!

You call this RAW?!? Here's a KNUCKLE SANDWICH for YOUR supper!!

Hey, you two! What's goin' ON up there?

I'LL tell you what's goin' on here, fight fans! Jerk lands a left to the eye an' the broad counters with a hard right to the ribs! Two quick jabs from Jerk sends her reeling, an' he closes in for the finish! Her legs are wobbly! She's down!!

57

Hey, Shmoey! Spare us the blow-by-blow, and just give us the RESULTS, okay . . . ?!
It's Jake . . . by a knockout!
I don't believe it! The old lady probably took a dive! She could KILL that bum if she wanted!
CHEESE
'You're an idiot for beatin' up on your Wife like that, Jerk! That's the worst thing you can do!
Why?? 'Cause she may pack up an' leave me??
No, cause you got a fight with Sugar Ray comin' up, an' you might ruin your hands!
Gee . . . I wish I cared about people the way YOU do, Shmoey!
It's somethin' you're either born with, or you ain't! From now on, use that CLUB I got you for your Wedding Present!!
Shmoey, you wanna do me a big favor? Start punchin' me in the face as hard as you can!
Anything you say, Jerk . . .
SPLATT
SOK
BAM
I know it gets boring between fights, Jerk, but one of these days you GOTTA learn how to collect stamps or paint by the numbers . . . like OTHER people!
Ain't this better than being punched in the face?!?
Yeah, it's great! A modern swimming pool . . . right in the heart of The Bronx! But, when does it get filled up with water?!?
Any minute now! It looks like rain!
Shmoey, who's that sexy blonde over there?
Her name is Vixen! But keep away from her, Jake! I hear she's big trouble!
Hi! If you ain't doin' nuthin,' whaddya say we kinda go over t' my place, have a couple of drinks, an' see what happens?
Well-l-l . . .
Uh—OKAY!
Boy, if there's ONE thing I CAN'T STAND, it's a TEASE!
HUBBA HUBBA

Pretty classy place, huh? But it's a little cluttered! I gotta throw some things out!
Le'me show you around, okay? This is my stove! This is my refrigerator!
This is my sink!
What's THIS?
This is his WIFE!
That's the FIRST THING I gotta throw out!
GOD BLAST OUR HOME
There's the chair! An' there's the dresser!
An' there's the BED . . .
Look, before you start anything, I want you to know I come from a good, respectable, religious family . . . and I never kiss on the first date!
I was thinkin' maybe we'd get undressed an' fool around!
Okay . . . but no kissing!!
Gee, Jerk, it was so fantastic . . . so terrific! Why'd you STOP?!?
I just remembered that I'm fightin' Sugar Ray tomorrow night! I NEVER have sex before a fight! If I have SEX, I can't concentrate on punchin' someone in the mouth!!
For YOU, punchin' someone in the mouth IS sex!!
I thought I threw her out!!
Well, this is IT! The big fight with Sugar Ray! Hey—is somethin' botherin' you, Jake?
That stupid, friggin' Wife of mine . . . that's what's botherin' me! She keeps tellin' me that boxin' is a substitute for SEX! Ain't that the most ridiculous thing you ever heard . . . ?!?
She's some dummy!!
Everyone KNOWS that boxin' is a business and sex is a pleasure!! Only a total idiot would mix 'em up!
BONNG!
FFFT
THUMP
Oh, MAN . . . the Earth really moved for me! How was it for you, Sugar Ray, baby?
It was just okay! I don't think it was as great for me as it was for you . . . !
Well, I'm pretty well rested now! Whaddaya say we try another round?
Not tonight . . . ! I got a headache!

Great news, Jerk! I finally got you that Title Fight with Cerdan! But there's a catch! First, you gotta fight some bum an' take a dive!
WHAT?! Are you kiddin'?! I never took no dive in my life, an' I ain't gonna start now!!
Listen, there's a HUNDRED GRAND in it for you!!
Whaddaya want . . . ? A swan . . . ? A jack-knife . . . ? I do a great belly-whop!!
GRAZIANO WINE
BOOOO! HISSS!
FIX!! FIX!
You're a BUM, LaMutha!
Would you explain something to me . . . ?
Sure! Just axe me . . .
How is LaMutha gonna remain the Number One Contender by losing this fight? Wouldn't the guy who BEATS him then become the Number One Contender?
Maybe ROBERTO DURAN is his strategist! It's obvious you don't understand the Fight Game!!
I lost it, Shmoey! I coulda killed 'im an' I lost it! I threw it! I took a dive . . . sob . . .
This is only the second time in his life I seen him cry!
When was the first?
The time he threw a left hook at our Mother . . . an' MISSED!
TONIGHT
ROCKY
BOXING
PENNIES
The years sure fly by fast, eh Jerk? You finally became Champ! You got a divorce, and you married Vixen! An' I got married, too! Ain't everythin' great?! What can possibly spoil it?
Off-hand, I can think of a couple of things! Like f'rinstance, if your Wife ever catches you with THIS broad!!
SPEAKIN' of foolin' aroun', do you think Vixen is cheatin' on me . . . ?
Look, you been buggin' me for days with that jealousy crap! I tell you she ain't foolin' aroun'! What makes you think she is?
The way every-body looks at her and seems to know her! Like THOSE guys, for example . . .
Hi, there, Vixen!
How's it goin'?
What's cookin', Baby?
MOUTH WASH
For God's Sake, Jerk! One of those guys is a PRIEST! The other is GAY!!
Yeah, but look how the THIRD ONE is look-in' at her!!
That's "COCKEYED" CAVELLO!! He's lookin' at ME!!

Panel 1:
I STILL think she's foolin' aroun'! Last week, when she got back from Atlantic City, she had this DOPEY GRIN on her face... like she'd had plenty of SEX!

You friggin' idiot! YOU were with her in Atlantic City!! You were on your HONEYMOON!

And I NEVER TOUCHED her!! I TOLD you she was foolin' aroun'!!

Panel 2:
Okay, you dirty two-timing broad!! Where WERE you?! Who were you MESSIN' AROUN' with?!? "HOT LIPS" HOROWITZ? "LOVER BOY" LUNDIGAN?!? "ROMEO" RICOTTA?!

F'r cryin' out loud!! I jus' took out the GARBAGE!! I was gone a minute and a half!

Panel 3:
You gotta stop wearin' yourself out like this, Jerk! Listen... you got a big return match with Sugar Ray comin' up! You gotta concentrate on that! You promise me you're gonna concentrate on nothin' but the Sugar Ray fight?

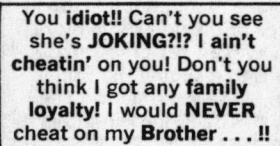

Okay... I promise...

Panel 4:
Way to go, Jerk!!

He's in terrific form!

I never SEEN him so sharp!!

Panel 5:
Now, you do that to SUGAR RAY, and you're a shoo-in!

You friggin' tramp! Take that n' that! THIS will teach you to cheat on ME!

I AIN'T cheatin' on you, you damn fool!!

Yes you are! C'mon! Tell me WHO you been cheatin' with, or I'll KILL ya...!

Okay, you really wanna know?! I'll tell you! I been cheatin' with Clark Gable, John Wayne, Haile Selassie, Pres. Truman, and your own brother, Shmoey!

My God! A friggin' ORGY!!

Panel 6:
You idiot!! Can't you see she's JOKING?!? I ain't cheatin' on you! Don't you think I got any family loyalty! I would NEVER cheat on my Brother...!!

That's RIGHT! I'm married to him, and I know Shmoey better than ANYBODY! He would NEVER cheat on his Brother! On his WIFE, maybe, but never his Brother!

Panel 7:
Boy, that LaMutha sure made a MESS out of his life!

Yeah! His own Brother walked out on him, his Wife hardly talks to him, and now, Sugar Ray is poundin' the crap outta him!

And look at the SHAPE he's in! You can't tell ME he's a Middleweight!

No?!? Take another look at his middle!

61

Panel 1: Y'know, Viven, I think I been hit in the **head** too many times! Here I am in a **black an' white** film—lookin' at **home** movies of us in **Florida** after I retire, an' they **look** like they're **IN COLOR!!**

Yeah! You think **THAT's** strange?! How about a **black and white** film with a **color home-movie sequence** in a **black an' white MAGAZINE?!?**

Panel 2: Since I **retired** from the **ring** and opened up this **night club**, things have been **great!** Plenty of **booze, broads** and **food** ... and lots of **laughs!**

Man, he musta put on **200 pounds!**

There's a rumor he's goin' into **Show Business!** Is it **true** he's gonna do "**The Odd Couple**"?!?

Yeah ... he's gonna play the **TITLE ROLE!**

Panel 3: Well, folks, I hate to eat an' **waddle**, but Vixen's waitin' for me out in the **car!** We've had our **problems** through the years, but she's been **loyal** to me ... right to the end ...!

Yeah ... she **stuck** by him through **thick an' THICKER!**

Panel 4: Hi, Hon! Sorry I'm so late ...

It **don'** matter no more, Jerk! It's all **over!** I'm **leavin'** you! **Forever!**

Look ... I'm **sorry** I've accused you of **cheatin'** on me all these years! I was **wrong!**

No, you were **right!** I **WAS** cheatin'! I been **seein'** someone on the **side** all along!!

What are you **talking** about?! He's **everything** you **ain't!** He's **sensitive** and **sweet** and **loved** and **respected!**

Yecccch! Sounds to me like you been seein' a **COLLEGE PROFESSOR!**

Panel 5: Next to **YOU**, he **IS** a College Professor!!

Panel 6: **Come back, Vixen! Please** come back!

He's just another pug! What can **HE** give you I can't?

Well, for **one** thing: financial security!! He's got at least **FIVE MORE** "Fight Pictures" in HIM!!

Hollywood's got about as **much chance** of making some **more money** on a fat creep like **YOU** with a **sequel** than they got making a sequel to "**The Attack Of The Killer Tomatoes**"!

VRROOOM

THE END

Limitations of being self-taught

"If I had it all to do over again," claims Drucker, "the only change I'd make would be attending art school or a university with a good art department. Being self-taught means being limited by your innate talent, personal experiences, and influences. You try to learn through imitation, and while some growth is possible in this manner, it depends upon the expertise of the artist that you emulate.

"Art teachers, professional instructors, and most of all your fellow students make you more aware of the *thinking* end of art which is a lot more difficult to learn by yourself. I went to Erasmus High School in Brooklyn, New York. There were no courses designed for the serious art student, so my parents encouraged me to attend art school after graduation. I tried Parsons School of Design for a while, but the emphasis was on art direction and similar areas far removed from what I was looking for."

There's a popular advertisement that reads: "I got my job through The New York Times"; Drucker did just that. His first professional art job came about by answering an "art assistant wanted" ad. Drucker worked on backgrounds for a syndicated strip for six months. He left because the job had no future, but he had learned enough about the field to land a new job in the art department of *National Periodicals*, where he worked for three years. Drucker's main duty there was to correct other artists' work. He had to imitate many styles and use varied techniques to keep his work consistent with the original. This also meant that he had to tackle many subjects comprising *National's* comic magazine line: western, adventure, love, war, and the cartoon features.

The constantly changing problems and varied styles involved were very helpful to this aspiring cartoonist; Drucker wanted to learn and broaden his art. He was later able to secure from the company free-lance assignments that he worked on at night and on weekends. As his work improved and became popular, Drucker was finally able to realize the first of his major goals by leaving salaried employment to become a fulltime free-lancer.

Drucker's greatest success was in a humorous line of comics featuring the fictional adventures of famous comedians: Bob Hope, Jerry Lewis, etc. His ability to capture these personalities with a few brushstrokes impressed editors and started him on the road to caricature. Now, Drucker needed an assistant, so his wife, Barbara, learned to wield the eraser and white-out paint.

As Drucker's markets broadened, so did his influence. When assigned straight illustrations for *Bluebook* and adventure and sport magazines, he found inspiration from the work of the leading illustrators of the day, Robert Fawcett and Austin Briggs. For humorous assignments he studied the action and exaggeration of Albert Dorne's figures. For caricature he turned to the work of Ronald Searle, the brilliant English artist, and Al Hirschfield, theatrical caricaturist in the Sunday *New York Times*. This amalgamation enabled Drucker's own personality to surface more confidently in a distinct style all his own.

(continued on p. 77)

THE OILY FIFTIES DEPT.

BOY ARE WE SICK AND TIRED OF MOVIES THAT TRY AND TELL US HOW MARVELOUS THINGS WERE BACK IN THE FIFTIES! ONCE AND FOR ALL, WE'D LIKE THEM TO....

Gee, Wizzo, I didn't think I'd see you **back** here this year!

I promised my folks I'd be a **Senior** by the time I was **thirty!** And I only missed by **three years!**

Hey, don't touch my **hair!** It's my key to **fame** and **fortune!**

Whadda ya mean?!?

Some guy from a **big company** saw me and offered me a **big contract!**

You mean like **Paramount Pictures??**

Nahh... **Standard Oil!** They said my hair should be good for at least **ten barrels a day!**

This year, I'm gonna turn over a **NEW LEAF!** I'm gonna take a **BATH** a lot more often!

Like **ONCE** a **DAY?**

I meant like **ONCE** a **SEMESTER!**

I seriously thought about **quitting** my job as a **Teacher** here and taking up **Alligator Wrestling** instead!

Why didn't you?

This is **much more** of a **CHALLENGE!**

Y'know, it's **funny!** Everything here is so **different!** Here, when it's **Winter**, it's **Summer** back home! When it's **daytime** here, it's **nighttime** there! Here you go **SOUTH** to get warm, there we go **NORTH!** Everything is just **opposite!**

You're **right!** What's exciting in **Australia** is very dull up here!

Like **What?**

Like **YOU!!**

Hey, whatchya doin', Dinny?

Practising for the big **Disco Contest** Saturday!

Schmuck! That's in **another picture!**

So **what's** the big **difference?!** I'm gonna do the **same kinda things** in **THIS one!!**

CEASE

ARTIST: MORT DRUCKER   WRITER: STAN HART

Panel 1:
- What did you do over the Summer, Sandee?
- I met a really nice guy! His lips drove me crazy!
- Why...?
- I'm wild about the taste of day-old Pizza!

Panel 2:
- I met a girl! She's really different from other girls!
- In what way?
- She was so bland and dull, she kept disappearing against the background!
- Dinny! What are you looking for?
- YOU! I can't see you when you stand in front of a sand dune!!

Panel 3:
- I sure hope you didn't do anything foolish with that boy last Summer!
- We did everything, but...!
- Everything, but... what?
- Everything, but... you know!!
- In YOUR case, it was probably just as well! Guys like to stay awake during... you know!

Panel 4:
- So... what are you majoring in this semester, Dinny?
- Remedial Reading!
- You oughta major in Remedial SINGING!
- Don't bug me! I'm worried enough about my Brother! He's quitting the Priesthood, and—
- Idiot! That problem's from your LAST movie!
- I know! But it's more interesting than any problem in THIS dopey movie!

65

Let me tell you about Summer love . . .
Started feelin' I was deep fried!
Started peelin'– lost half my hide!
Blisters, sun rash! I never tanned!
Lost all my cash in the damn sand!
Sun burn blotch!
Sand up your crotch!
Ain't no fun in Summer love!!
Dinny! It's you!!
Sandee!!
I called, and your parents said you moved away from home!
Ahh, they only said that to protect their property value!
Then I looked for you on the beach . . . and I thought you'd drowned!
Why'd you think that?
I saw an oil slick on the ocean!
Isn't it lucky we met again?!
Lucky for us, but not for this picture!
How come?
Because we had our big emotional scenes in the first two minutes! What's left?!?
Let's think of a problem to keep this movie moving!
How about me wanting to leave Brooklyn to go live in Manhattan?
Why do you keep going back to your last movie?
I want to FORGET!!
But you keep remembering your PAST!!
I know! It's the present I want to forget!
The guys are watchin' me! I better be mean and cruel to her . . .
Hey, chick! Get lost!
Why is he so cruel to me?
He's embarrassed to have the guys think he's in love with a girl!
And it's less embarrassing if they think he's in love with a GUY?!?

I got an offer to go into films!
Yeah!! VD films! for the Army!
I admire Wizzo for staying in school!
Yeah! She's staying until graduation or menopause, whichever comes first!!
Here am I, I'm apple pie; Wholesome 'til the day I die; There is no doubt; This dish just won't make out; This dish is apple pie!
It's for sure I'm virgin pure; And I'll never take the cure; I'll just say "Nope!"– And be like Ivory Soap; Forever virgin pure!
Are you making fun of me?
I didn't know you were there!
Will you please stop standing in front of white walls!
Kenocker, I'll give you everything, but . . .!
Everything, but what??
Everything, but resistance!
Oh, Kenocker, you sure are terrific at making love!!
Don't thank him . . .!
. . . Thank me!!
Get outta here, Cragface, and leave us alone!
I just wanted to see how that sloppy beat-up old heap could take it!
Hey, nobody talks about my car that way!!
I was talking about your date!!
Oh, that's different!
BAM! BAM!
Whatchya doin' with him?!?
He's an athlete! Or, as you say in America . . . a "Yock"!
That's "JOCK"!
He's wonderful! He can do anything you can do, and more!! Much more!
Yeah? Can he give a car a complete lube job, just by rubbing his head on the engine block?!

68

Panel 1:
Dog-gie School drop out! All the dogs were smarter than you! Dog-gie School drop out! You couldn't do what doggies do!

You failed "fetch" and "sit" and even "heel"! And now, they're all complaining! You left school in such and awful mess, When you flunked "paper training"!

That **does** it! I'm gonna go where no one will NOTICE how stupid I am! I'm going **back** to Riddle High!

Gee, her problem gets solved almost as fast as Dinny and Sandee's!

Panel 2:
I've been **thinking**, Dinny! There are **two** things **I** can't do! One is to keep running after you! The other is hang around with those dumb girls!

Hey, there's **another** thing you can't do!

What? DANCE!!

Panel 3:
Hello, Dinny! I've **missed** you! Remember when we used to **bounce** on my **bed**?!?

When you were **kids** together??

I'm talking about when we **made out** together!!

Well, it's time to **get angry** at you again, Dinny! Good-bye!!

WANNA DANCE?

Panel 4:
... and the winners are Dinny and Cha Cha!

They get a **trophy** for being the **best dancers**, and **fifty dollars** for oiling the gym floor!

I think the **Puerto Rican** couple shoulda won!

I think you better **forget** your last movie and **try** to salvage **THIS** one!!

Panel 5:
It's about time I got a problem of **my own** in this flick!

Hey, Kenocker, I think I'm **pregnant**! But don't breathe a word of this to **anybody**!

YOU'RE PREGNANT

Panel 6:
Hey! Wizzo's knocked up!

Oh-oh! I'm leavin' town!

The **whole** town is leavin' town!!

Why'd you have to do **THAT** for!?

I never saw a stampede before!

What'll this do to my **reputation**?! Confirm it!!

69

You really think you can beat Cragface in a car race . . .?
Sure! I'll burn rubber when I start . . . zig-zag around the traffic lights . . . cut him off. . . and ram him!
Think you can do all that??
Why not?! I DID IT on my Driver's Test!!
Amazing! I never saw anything like that!!
Ahhh, I see that kind of thing plenty!
Really? When??
When the kids try to get a spot in the High School parking lot!!
You won, Dinny! You won!
You're fabulous, Dinny! Make out with me!
Make out with ME!
No, ME!
Sorry! I'm saving myself till I'm married!
And when you're married?
THEN, I'll make out with ALL of you!!
I love him, and I'm going to change for him! That's the moral in this movie! In order to get the guy you love . . .
You have to be a SLUT!! What a wonderful message for the youth of America!!
Hi, there, Stud! What's happenin'?
You bet your buns, lover!
Oh, wow, Sandee! Is that YOU?!
That's fantastic! Just a minute ago, you were a dull, bland virgin! Now, you're a dull, bland slut!
Guess what, Kenocker! I'm not pregnant!
Ahhh, who cares!!
These were the fif-ties, when
Things were really great and
Folks weren't goin' nuts!
Kids then were nifties, with
Girls in clingy sweaters and
Guys in duck-tail hair cuts!
Life was a
Saturday night prom date!
That's the way it was then!
But we won't men-tion the
People like McCarthy and
Crazies like him around!
And Cold War tension, with
War in South Korea and
Bomb shelters underground!
Things now are
A helluva lot better
Than the way it was then!

KISSY-KISSY, BANG-BANG DEPT.

We hear that a lot of Italian-American Societies are up in arms over a recent motion picture because it casts a slur against honest, upstanding Italian-Americans. And we can understand their position. But what we *can't* understand is why a lot of Hollywood Societies aren't up in arms over this movie... because it casts a slur against honest, upstanding Movie-Makers. You'll see what we mean as we present this MAD version of...

THE BROTHER HOODS

ARTIST: MORT DRUCKER   WRITE: LOU SILVERSTONE

Hey, get your **holy statues** of Frank Costello!

Hey, get your **color slides** of Lucky Luciano's funeral... the **only authorized** photos taken!

Hey, get your **official L.P. record** of Joe Valachi... singing before the **Senate Committee**!

It's **him**! It's the **Americano**!

You mean the one who came to kill Frank Gilletta?

No, the one who came to kill **this picture**!

He's **here**, Signore Gilletta... a well-dressed, clean-cut, Madison Ave. Jr. Executive type with horn-rimmed glasses!

Sounds like your **typical Syndicate Triggerman** to me! Is he acting **suspicious**?

Chi lo sa?! Who knows!? He's such a **lousy actor**, I can't tell!

Lousy actor!? Hey, **that's** no Syndicate Triggerman! That's my **brother**!!

Krankie! *Battelo a me!*

Vengie! *Qui anda il Giudice!*

Mamma Mia! It's the "Kiss of Death"!

What "Kiss of Death"!? Don't you ever go to the **movies**? That's the latest craze... boys kiss boys... and girls kiss girls!

Yecch! Bring back the **good ol' days**!

La penna sulla tavola non é di mia zia, é di mio zio!

Vengie! This **is** a surprise! What are **you** doing here in Sicily?

I was in the **neighborhood** so I dropped by to see if you **needed** anything!

I'll **tell** you what I need— **SUB-TITLES**!! I can't understand a word we're **saying** in this movie!

71

Aida! Look who's here! It's Vengie!
Hey, is that all the luggage you brought?
Actually, I just stopped in for a bit to eat, Krank! I hate to hit and run . . . I mean EAT and run, but . . .
Did you hear that, woman? Vengie just dropped by to join us for supper!
Something tells me it's gonna be your LAST SUPPER, Krank . . . unless that's his toothbrush he just dropped!
CLUNK!
Wait, I'll ask him! Er, Vengie! Vengie . . . ? Hey, what's the matter?
Don't disturb him, Krankie! He's trying to remember the past!
Oh, I thought he was trying to remember his line!
Your brother is lucky to get a girl like my Enema. Just by looking at her, you can tell she's built to have plenty of bambinos!
Your Enema is lucky to get a guy like my brother! He's got a great future!
Where? In the Mafia?
Where else? In the movies? An actor, he's not!
This is a beautiful wedding, Vengie . . . but that centerpiece!
Gee, Enema! That's a gift from my brother, Krankie! He had it shot especially for the occasion!
Salvatore, you stupido pig! Get offa the table! That ain't your seat! And can't you wait for everybody else before you start-a to eat?! Contadino ignorante Siciliano!
Mamma mia, hó un mal di testa Excedrin!
Well, kid! What are your plans?
I want to come in with you, Krankie!
I'm glad you feel that way, Vengie! I need somebody like you in the business!
You mean somebody you can trust?
No . . . I mean somebody who can talk English!
Now, the first thing on Monday morning . . .
Hold it, Krankie! Take it easy! I'm just married!
Okay, TUESDAY morning . . .

Panel 1:
— Vengie! Vengie! **Why?** Why do you want to get into the **rackets?**
— You're a **college man!** What do **you** know about **violence** and **bloodshed?**
— **Don't forget!** I went to **Columbia!**

Panel 2:
— **All right!** Have it your **own way!** Only never tell me what you **do!** I don't want to hear how you get your **blood money!**
— Gee... I didn't know you felt so **strongly** about it!
— Well, I **do!** Now pass me the **Real Estate Section** so I can find us a $250,000 brownstone in Brooklyn Heights!
— Then we'll have to go to **Paris** to pick out the furniture for it!

Panel 3:
— Oh, Mr. Gilletta! **Thank you** for coming to Salvatore's funeral! He owed you **so much!** Why, he wouldn't **be** where he is today if it weren't for **you!**
— Hey, **Eduardo!** How come you spit in Salvatore's casket? Didn't you **like him?**
— **Sure** I like him! But they gotta no **spittoons** in here! You want I should spit on the **rug?**

Panel 4:
— Listen, Murray! We're in the **same Syndicate**, right? So how come **I** live in a crumby two-story walk-up in Brooklyn, and **you** live in a swanky joint like this?
— Because Krankie, **you** got a *Goyisher kopf!*
— Hey, *gumba!* That's the first Italian I understood in this picture!

Panel 5:
— Okay! Let's vote on the motion that the Syndicate **take over** the United States Government!
— I vote "NO!"
— Why, Krankie? What's **wrong** with the idea?
— I may have a *Goyisher kopf*, Murray, but it don't take a **genius** to know that the U.S. Government **loses** money every year! Who needs **that** headache?

Panel 6:
— The—*hic*—the shtoopid zipper is—*hic*—shtuck! Hol' shtill—*hic*—an' I'll **shoot** it open!
— Tell me something, Krankie! If this whole flashback is taking place in your brother's **mind**, how come he knows what happened here in our **bedroom?**
— Now you know **why** the Mafia is called a **"SECRET Society"!**

73

Antonio Mozzarella! Luigi Lasagna! Mario Marinara! Guiseppe Linguini! Alphonso Ziti! Carmine Calamari!
Do you know these **names,** Krankie?
Sure! Those are the names of the **men** the **Syndicate knocked off!**
No, those are the names of our **all-time great Bocci team!**
But we **do** know who squealed on your **Papa,** Krankie! It was **Duminick Bertololo!**
You gotta make him **pay!** You gotta **kill** him, Krankie!
But Bertololo is **family!** He's my brother's **Father-in-Law!** How come you waited **30 years** to tell me?
We just **found out today!** Our informant forgot to put the **zip code** on the **envelope!**
. . . and this Gilletta is a **known Syndicate man** and **labor racketeer!** He is guilty of **murder . . . extortion . . . smuggling . . . loan sharking . . .**
Oh, Papa! Is it **true** what that Senator is **saying** about you?
Who you gonna **believe** . . . your own **Papa** . . . or some **U.S. Senator?!** You **know** those bums in Washington are all **crooks!**
Besides, why do you watch **THAT** garbage? Why don't you watch **something worthwhile** . . . like re-runs of **"The Untouchables"!?**
Now go do your homework! And if your report card doesn't **improve,** I'm gonna put out a contract on your **teacher** . . . even if she **IS** a **Nun!**
Imagine, giving my baby an **"F"** in **"Social Studies"!**
BLESS
OUR
COSA
NOSTR
Hey, Bertololo! I changed my **mind** about that **U.S. Government take-over!** Get in! Let me buy you a lunch!
Now you're **talking sense,** Krankie! But why are you parked near a **fire hydrant?** You want the **cops** to pick you up?
WHAT cops? You see any **cops** in this picture? This is a **true-to-life picture** about the **Syndicate . . .** and you **know** that, as far as the **Syndicate** is concerned, **cops** just **don't exist!**
Hey, remember the time I had a contract on **Angie LaBonza,** and I shot his **brother** by mistake? *Ha-ha!* The organization got a **bargain** that time, eh, Dum? **Two hits** for the price of **one!**
And remember the time I shot **Tony Brazzioli** in front of **witnesses**—*heh-heh!*—and they picked up some idiot named **Frank Gorshin?**
Heh-heh! Oh, Krankie—you —*heh-heh*— **kill** me!
That's **right,** fink! As soon as we get where we're **going!**

Panel 1:
- "Hey, Krankie! Why'd you go to all that trouble to tie him up so he **strangles** himself! Why don't you just **shoot** him?"
- "Because this is a Ritual Murder... and I gotta do it according to the 'Ritual Murder Manual'! And it says right here.. 'Double-crossers get **shot**!', 'Swindlers get packed in **cement** and dropped in **rivers**!'... and 'Squealers get tied up so they **strangle** themselves!'"

Panel 2:
- G-A-A-A-K!
- M-M-M-F-F-!
- C-H-O-K-E!
- "This scene will probably get the picture an 'S' Rating!"
- "What does an 'S' Rating mean?"
- "It means, 'Nobody Under 18 Admitted Unless Accompanied By A Sadist!'"

Panel 3:
- "I say, 'Hit!'"
- "Yeah, 'Hit!'"
- "'Hit!'"
- "You heard the **vote**, Vengie! You gotta hit your **brother**!"
- "Okay, I'll **do** it! I'll give him such a **hit**! I'll give him a left to the **eye**... No, a right to the **mouth**..."
- "*Managgia!* Whose idea **was** it to bring College Men into the Organization?!"

Panel 4:
- "Okay, Vengie! Enough 'flashbacking'! We got business! Right?"
- "Right! So turn around... and I'll blow your brains out!"
- "Hold it! We gotta do this according to **tradition**! First we gotta have a 'Cousins' Club Picnic'!"
- "A 'Cousins' Club Picnic'!? I dunno! I think I'd rather have MY brains blown out!!"

Panel 5:
- "First, we **dance**!"
- "Listen, two guys **kissing** was bad enough! But this—"

Panel 6:
- "Then we **eat**!"
- "Funny things about Sicilian food! An hour after you **eat** it, you're **dead**!"

Panel 7:
- "...and then we **drink**!!"
- "Boy, this sure beats getting zapped in a **dark alley**, or in a **junkyard** in Jersey!"

75

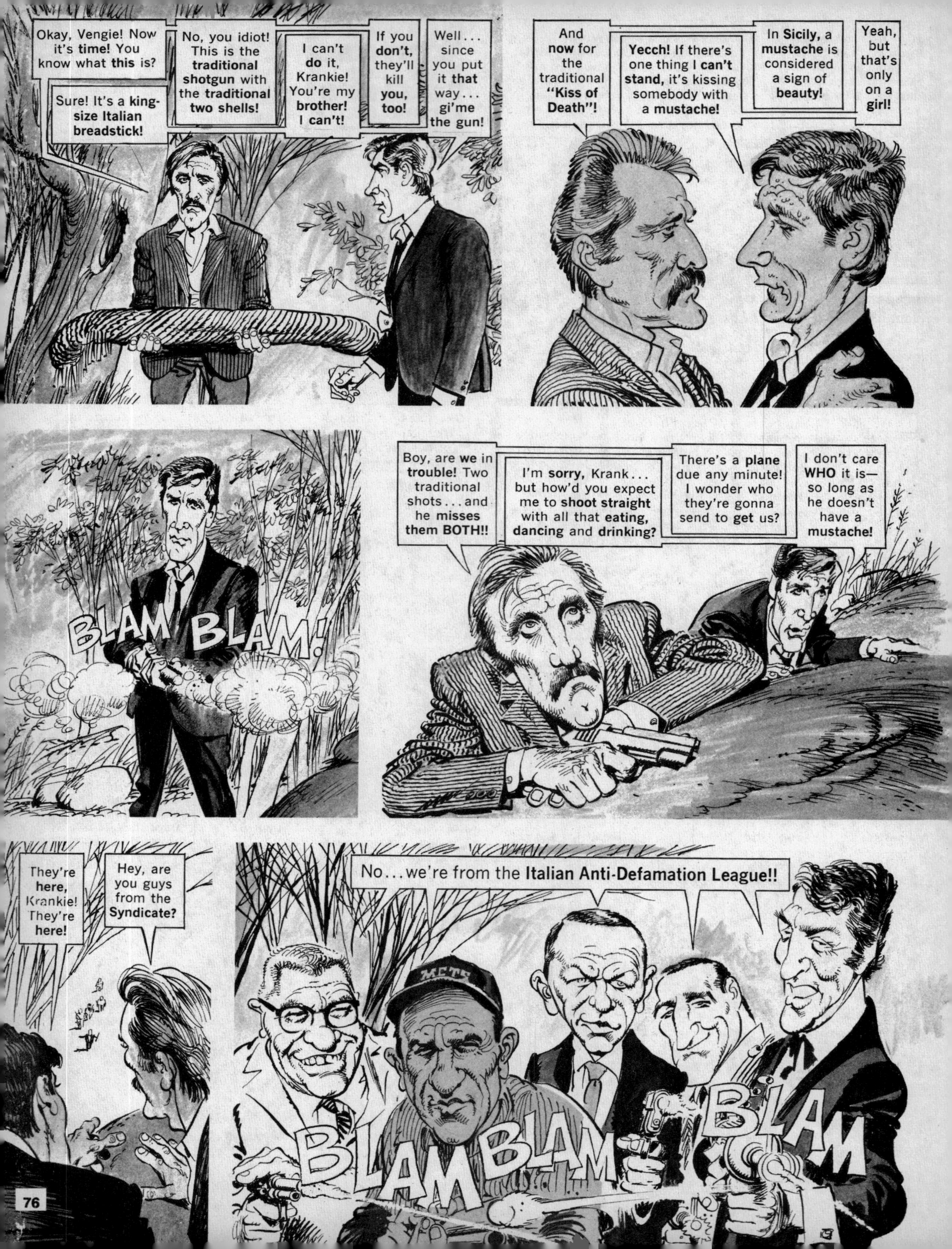

Okay, Vengie! Now it's time! You know what this is?
Sure! It's a king-size Italian breadstick!
No, you idiot! This is the traditional shotgun with the traditional two shells!
I can't do it, Krankie! You're my brother! I can't!
If you don't, they'll kill you, too!
Well... since you put it that way... gi'me the gun!
And now for the traditional "Kiss of Death"!
Yecch! If there's one thing I can't stand, it's kissing somebody with a mustache!
In Sicily, a mustache is considered a sign of beauty!
Yeah, but that's only on a girl!
BLAM BLAM!
Boy, are we in trouble! Two traditional shots... and he misses them BOTH!!
I'm sorry, Krank... but how'd you expect me to shoot straight with all that eating, dancing and drinking?
There's a plane due any minute! I wonder who they're gonna send to get us?
I don't care WHO it is— so long as he doesn't have a mustache!
They're here, Krankie! They're here!
Hey, are you guys from the Syndicate?
No... we're from the Italian Anti-Defamation League!!
BLAM BLAM BLAM BLAM

Working directly

Drucker doesn't think out his ideas on paper. He doesn't do thumbnail sketches. He prefers instead to envision the completed work in his mind beforehand. He later duplicates the concept on paper as best he can, allowing accidents and changes that may possibly improve the work as he goes along. Drucker finds drawing directly and committing his idea to paper in a one-time hit-or-miss approach can generate more excitement and originality than permitting the pencil to wander over the page in search of a visual solution to the problem. "It's also a sure way to keep from being too influenced by your research," reveals Drucker. "I put the figure in where I think it belongs and not where the photo dictates. Staging an illustration around available reference points limits your freedom to tell a story effectively; when an artist does that, he ignores his very purpose."

Working directly is not necessarily a timesaving procedure. While the composition is thought out carefully, not all inherent problems are obvious from the start, nor are they easily solved cerebrally. The artist must still work diligently to transfer mental image to working surface. This can be just as (if not more) time-consuming as doing a series of rough preparatory sketches.

One of the most important factors in direct drawing is *selectivity*. In humorous illustration, especially, care must be taken to clarify the point or message of the work. Extraneous material, no matter how well drawn or how attractively executed, will hurt more than help the drawing if not handled subtly. Anything that calls attention away from the main focus or distracts the reader is best underplayed or left out entirely. Drucker will sometimes use pencil, for example, to illustrate the background of a panel, while executing the foreground figures or the composition's focal point in pen. The tonal washed-out quality of the pencil work serves almost as a backdrop for the action at center stage.

Pen, ink, and radio

Drucker prefers to work on 2- or 3-ply Strathmore illustration board. The heavier stock permits extensive use of washes and transparent color, the artist's favorite methods, with a minimum of paper buckling. The high-quality finish also allows for frequent erasures without spoiling the surface of the paper—a very necessary consideration for most artists who prefer to work directly.

Drucker is essentially a pen man, preferring the Gillott line of flexible pen nibs for their ease and constant flow. He does not care for the rigid quality of crowquill points. He finds they dig into the paper, spatter, and do not move as easily across the page when a quick, flowing line is desired. He has found Artone's Fine Line India ink to be well-suited to his penwork, switching over to Artone Extra-Dense black for large areas to be brushed on with a Winsor & Newton #2 or #3 red sable watercolor brush.

Drucker did most of his early color work with colored pencils that can dilute and mix with water. He then began using Pelikan colored inks in addition to the pencils. Ultimately, he used the inks almost exclusively (with perhaps a few touches of diluted pencil for special effects). Dr. Martin's dyes were then added to the palette and, finally, Winsor & Newton watercolors in solid form (at this writing, this is the artist's favorite color technique).

His radio is "as important as my drawing equipment," declares Drucker. "I always work with it playing in the background. Most of the time I'm not even aware I'm listening. It's just a way of touching the world outside while putting in long hours of relative isolation. But then, months later when I see my work in print, I can recall exactly what I was listening to when I penciled in this head or inked in that figure. It's a crazy way to remember things. I only wish it worked as well for remembering birthdays and anniversaries!"

Objectivity

Drucker tries to remain objective when drawing his subjects. Yielding to the temptation to compliment those you admire or be purposely unflattering to those you don't will limit your artistry. Any obvious or heavy-handed attempt at ridicule will insult your audience, even those of similar persuasion. Actually, you may end up defeating your own aim. There's a "root for the underdog" attitude prevalent in this country. An "I don't like the other guy, either, but that's going too far" response to your work that might be all that's needed to push someone over to the other side.

A caricaturist is also a journalist. With the exception of political cartoons, he's responsible more for reportage than opinion. Respecting the readers' intelligence and allowing them to form their own opinions is always the most effective educational process.

(continued page 115)

CREEP IN THE HEART OF TEXAS DEPT.

TV programs about families have always been popular! The Nelsons, the Waltons, the Bradfords, the Ingles, the Cunninghams, etc., all these families had certain things in common: they were all happy, they all loved each other, and none of them had very much money! Now, a different type of TV family has emerged to capture the top ratings. These people are more like the Borgias than the Bradfords! These people hate each other, they're miserable, and they're filthy rich! Yep, we're talking about that nighttime "soap" about a typical Texas family, soaking in depravity and sex! Boy, when it comes to remembering that there are finer things in life, all that base immorality on the TV screen tends to numb us, to deaden us, to—

DU

I'm J. D. Phewing! I'm mean, corrupt, dishonest, evil and loathsome! And those are my GOOD qualities! My downright nastiness has made me the most popular character on TV, except for maybe Miss Piggy!

I'm J. D.'s Brother, Wary! I'm a snivelling weak coward—and it's all J. D.'s fault! When we were kids, he used to break all my toys—and torture me! And that was when he was being NICE to me!! When I got married, HE went on the honeymoon . . . with my wife!!

My name is Juicy! Wary is my Daddy! At least I think he is! I'm a typical Texas co-ed! I'm majoring in Advanced Sex, Partying, Adultery and Twirling!

I'm Sullen Phewing, J.D.'s beloved—*hah*—Wife! J.D. tried to have me committed a couple of times just because I'm an alcoholic nymphomaniac with paranoid-schizophrenic tendencies! Luckily, my behavior was considered normal for a nighttime soap!

Hi! I'm J.D.'s baby Brother, Booby! I'm a decent, moral person! I'm rather intelligent, and I'm normal in all respects! In other words, I'm the family SCHMUCK!

I'm Booby's Wife, Spamella Phewing! That snake, J.D., was responsible for me having a miscarriage! He ruined my father, destroyed my Brother's career, and—worst of all—cut the LABELS off my designer jeans!!

LLUS

I'm Nelly Phewing... and this is my Husband, **Jerk**! We're the **proud parents** of these fine specimens of Dullus manhood! Last season, my Son, **J.D.** was **shot**, and a **lot** of folks thought that maybe **I** did it! Now, **that's** downright embarrassing! I mean, if I'd **shot** J.D., I **wouldn't** have just **WOUNDED HIM!**

You may be wond'rin' why all the Phewing ladies are wearin' **FUR COATS** to this **outdoor barbecue** when the **weather** here in Texas is **110°** in the shade! Well, we Phewings are **SO RICH**, the **ENTIRE RANCH** is air conditioned!

Score cards! Get your **score cards** here! You **can't keep track** of **who's scoring** with **who** without a **score card!!**

Mornin' y'all! Sorry I'm late, but a **Girl Scout** came to the door and I swindled her out of her **cookies!** And **then** I had to break up a **romance** between **Roy Greppser** and **Donna Pulverson!**

Roy and **WHO?!?**

Donna! You remember! **Sam Pulverson's Widow!** He was involved in that **shady oil lease deal** with me and **Cess Pool**, who was married to **Messy!** She's the gal who was **cheatin'** with **Wary** after he married **Valvoline** who was runnin' around with lawyer **Phil Kleindingst!**

By God, I **can't** keep track of these people! I **shoulda** bought me one of them **score cards** in the last panel!!

ARTIST: MORT DRUCKER   WRITER: LOU SILVERSTONE

I've got some **GOOD NEWS!** **Juicy** has got herself engaged!

Well, now! That **IS** good news!

I—I can't believe it! You're **HAPPY** I'm engaged?!

Of course I am, Darlin'! I'm lookin' forward to the pleasure of **breakin'** it up, then **destroyin'** your fiancee and his entire family, including pets! But even worse than that, I'm gonna **TELL** you when your **Bridal Shower** is ... and **RUIN** your **SURPRISE!**

SCORING

79

Panel 1:
- May I be excused?
- Why? Got some last minute homework t' do?!?
- No, I have some last minute making out t' do! This isn't "Eight Is Enough," y'know! Besides, I can't take these family meals! The Last Supper had to be a laugh riot compared to eating with the Phewings!
- Hold on there, young lady! We all ENJOY these family meals! Why, jus' look at the SMILE on Mama's face!
- WHAT smile?!? That's GAS!!

Panel 2:
- Since you obviously aren't MAN enough to give Daddy a Grandson like I did, Booby, I'd like to offer my services to help you out!
- Why, that's right nice of you, J.D.... wantin' to help out your little Brother that way!
- Jus' cause your Wife had a BABY doesn't mean that you're the Father, J.D.! Not with YOUR Wife, it don't!

Panel 3:
- By God, J.D.... you shouldn't let anyone talk bad about your Wife like that! Why, if anybody dared say that about your Mama, I'd kill 'im!
- So would I, Daddy! Nobody better say anythin' bad about Mama while I'M around!
- Dammit, J.D.! For once, be a man! When somebody insults your Wife's honor, DO somethin'!
- All right, Daddy! If that's what you want, then that's what I'll do! Just watch me!!
- (sign: KILL GUN CONTROL)
- (buttons: BIG GUN / SON OF GUN)

Panel 4:
- Now hear this!! If I find out that anybody's messin around with my Wife, I'll KILL HIM!!
- BLAM! BLAM!
- Hi Yo Silver! Away!
- Gittum up Scout!
- Who was that masked man?!?

Panel 5:
- Sullen, I don't want you goin' around, casting doubts about me bein' the Father of our baby! Why, do you know what people are callin' me...??
- The same thing they're callin' the baby, I imagine!
- Y'know, he's a cute lil' devil! I can't see how anyone can say I'm not his Daddy! He LOOKS jus' like me... an' he even ACTS jus' like me sometimes!
- Only when he gets diaper rash!

Panel 6:
- Hmmm! Next week is Booby's birthday! I gotta do somethin' real special for him! I know!! I'll break up his marriage...!
- Dammit, Spam! Our marriage is fallin' apart! Now, I KNOW you don't want to have a BABY... but puttin' on RUBBER GLOVES to shake hands with me is goin' jus' a lil' too far!!

Panel 1:
- Well, it's **not** all **MY** fault our marriage is failing!! How about **YOU** and this **HENNA MAID**!?
- I **TOLD** you!! There's **nothing** between us! Henna is just an **old school chum**!
- Yeah? Well, don't hold any more **CLASS REUNIONS** here in **our bed**!!
- The eyes of Texas are upon you—

Panel 2:
- Come to think of it, **WHY** would I want to break up that marriage?
- Grandma, the Phewings are **so rich** and **beautiful**!! How come everybody is **so miserable**??
- That's 'cause the TV audience **enjoys** seeing rich people **suffer**! It makes their **OWN** dull lives seem **more tolerable**!

Panel 3:
- Would you believe my image is being **ruined** by that **hockey puck** wearing a Roy Rogers hat... that **yo-yo** who walks like his **jockey shorts** are twisted?!? Thanks to **THAT** dummy, people think **I'M A NICE GUY**!!
- Compared to **him**, we're **ALL** considered nice guys!!

Panel 4:
- J.D., I've got to talk to you!!
- Lowland, this better be **important**! I don't like being **disturbed** when I'm doing important business like interviewing some new Secretaries!!
- **Secretaries?!?** They look more like **Dullus Cheerleaders**!
- On this show, all the gals look like **Dullus Cheerleaders**!
- Gi'me a J...
- Gi'me a D...
- Gi'me a **PHEW**!
- Gi'me an **ING**!

Panel 5:
- Our **project** converting the **John Wayne Memorial Park** into a **real estate development** has hit a snag! The **Alamo Sisterhood Society** has **vowed** to stop us! They're threatening to **chain** themselves to the statue of Roger Staubach...!!
- Of course, we **COULD** use the **LAW**, and have them removed **LEGALLY**!
- **LEGALLY?** You must be **KIDDING**! Are you trying to ruin my reputation?!

Panel 6:
- That's no problem! A.S.S. is a group of **ladies**, right?! I'll just turn on the old **Phewing** charm and seduce the gal in charge!
- Uh... the Leader of the group is your Wife, Sullen!!
- Well... now we **DO** have a problem! That's the **ONE** lady in Texas that I **CAN'T** sweet talk into bed!
- Hold it! Hey, I think I've got it...

81

Panel 1:
- Dr. Smelby, I need your help!
- Frankly, Phewing, I **don't** even think **FREUD** could help you!! But I'll give it my **best shot!** What do these **remind** you of?
- That one makes me think of **money**... and that one looks like a guy running a stampeding herd over his **family!**

Panel 2:
- I don't want **THAT** kind of help, Doc!! I want you to **commit** my Wife! I've got **PROOF** she's crazy!!
- This is just your **MARRIAGE LICENSE!**
- **What woman** in her right mind would marry **ME!?!**
- Good Lord, you're **right!** She **IS** stark raving mad! I'll have her put away **immediately!**

Panel 3:
- Lowland, didn't my new Secretary tell you I'm in **CONFERENCE**... and I **can't** be disturbed?!
- J.D., honey, **I'M** your new Secretary!
- Sorry, J.D., but this is important! Your wife's replacement as head of A.S.S.'s "Committee To Save The Park" is your **Mother!**
- I guess that means I got to get rid of **Mama!!**

Panel 4:
- J.D.!! You **wouldn't**... I mean... not even **YOU**...!!!
- Kill Mama?! Lord, no! Texas juries don't mind you killin' your **business partner**, your **wife**, or even a **total stranger!** But they **DO** frown on anybody bumpin' off his **Mama!** Why, that's almost as bad as bein' **mean** to your **horse!!**

Panel 5:
- Mama, Daddy, I been thinkin'! Why don't you two take a li'l **vacation?** I'll look after the ranch while you're away!
- **Hah!** The last time we left you in charge, you **mortgaged** the ranch, caused 3 miscarriages, 2 divorces, 5 suicides, 4 bankruptcies, broke up 12 couples—including our prize heifer and bull—and, **worst** of all, you didn't feed my **GOLDFISH!!**
- I did, **TOO**, Mama! I fed 'em to the **CAT!!**

Panel 6:
- And don't forget what you did to your **poor Brother**, Wary! You drove him clean off the South Pork to **KNUTT'S LANDING!!**
- Mama, I **did** it for his **own** good! Now, he's got a show of his **own!** Why, I even go there once in a while to see how he's doin'!!
- You **only** go there to torment the po'r boy!
- Yeah, but havin' me as a "guest villain" once in a while sure does **wonders** for his **NEILSEN RATINGS!**

I'm afraid I can't leave now, J.D.! I'm in charge of The A.S.S. Committee To Save The Park!
I didn't know you were so interested in preserving nature!
What nature?!? I'm interested in preserving our life style! They plan to put up condominiums that will sell for half a million each! We can't let low-down trash like that move into our neighborhood!
You don't have to worry, Mama! I'LL see to it that nothing happens to your park while you're away! Scout's Honor!
Maybe we SHOULD go, Nelly! I'd like to visit New Mexico! I've been thinkin' of buyin' some land!
What PART of New Mexico?
The WHOLE STATE?
Joke, don't you think J.D. seemed kind of anxious to get rid of us? Packin' our bags and makin' us peanut butter and jelly sandwiches like that?!?
You're too suspicious, Miss Nelly! Anyway, he promised to see that the park would be safe! He even gave you his "Scout's Honor"!!
I know! But remember! J.D. was the only Boy Scout who ever earned a Merit Badge for LYING!!
SOUTHPORK R
TOM LANDRY for PRES.
DARREL ROYAL for GOV.
Miss Nelly, I think we've got to TRUST J.D. on this!
WHY . . . ? Because he's our SON . . . ?!
No . . . because in order for his ridiculous, underhanded schemes to WORK, people have to TRUST him, even though they end up gettin' SCREWED EVERY TIME!!
Good work, J.D.! With Miss Nelly gone, the opposition collapsed! We'll make a fortune on this!
Now that's funny! I thought you said "WE"! Didn't I tell you—this entire project belongs to me!
There goes J.D., pullin' another double-cross on poor ol' Lowland!
No wonder he got shot!
I cain't understand all the fuss over the shootin' of one varmint! Especially here in TEXAS!!
Hell, Hopalong Cassidy, Matt Dillon and The Lone Ranger used to shoot DOZENS of people every week, and nobody ever thought a thing about it!
PLUNDER DEVELOPE INC.
why, J.D., you lousy crook! You'd swindle your own Mother!
I DID, a few panels back! Now, it's your turn! Lowland, I've got some information that'd RUIN you if I made it public!!
Forget it, J.D.! You can't blackmail me! Everybody KNOWS that I cheat on my wife, gamble, and swindle my depositors! I'm trying to get my own series!

Listen to this . . .
I've got this real deep dark secret, Doctor Smelby . . .
It's a tape of one of my sessions with my SHRINK!!
What'd you expect? Dolly Parton?
YOU WIN, J.D.! I'll do anything! I'll SIGN AWAY anything! Please! Just give me that tape! PLEASE!!
TEXAS INSTRUMENT
Just put your signature on these papers, Lowland! They make you the HEAD of this Real Estate Development!
But . . . WHY are you putting ME in charge?
So you can go to jail when I cheat all the customers! But look at the bright side, Lowland! In jail, you'll be safe! My Mama won't be able to get her hands on you, 'cause she's gonna be awful mad when she sees what you did to her park!
Hey, J.D., what was on that tape that made him cave in so easily?
Ol' Lowland confessed to Doc Smelby that he rooted for the STEELERS over the COWBOYS in the Super Bowl!!
No wonder! Man, we'll tolerate a lot of things here in Texas: murder, embezzlement, adultery! But THAT's goin' a li'l TOO FAR!
Mr. Phewing, there're some people from WASHINGTON to see you!
I'll be right there, Darlin'!
Man, that J.D. really knows how to live!! A PHONE and a BAR in his car!
That's the way it goes with some people! First, a MAGIC BOTTLE . . . now an EMPIRE!!
J.D. we're from the "Concerned America Party!" After the last election, we realized that we can't depend on conventions and primaries to get us the kind of man we need in the White House!
We would be honored if you'd be our Presidential Candidate for 1984!!
I'm flattered, and it would make my Mama mighty proud . . . but . . . WHY ME?!?
At this point in history, we need a leader who is as underhanded and conniving as the Russians . . . and as scheming and devious as the OPEC countries!
And YOU, J.D., are THAT MAN!!
Yes, sir! With J.D. Phewing wheeling and dealing in the oval office, the U.S.A. would be NUMBER ONE again!

A STAR IS PORN DEPT.

ARTIST: MORT DRUCKER   WRITER: PAUL LAIKIN

MAD'S X-RATED CELEBRITY TRIVIA QUIZ

Fill In The Blanks. Answers Below.

1. Despite his fame as a lover, Burt Reynolds suffers from premature _____.
2. On their wedding night, Prince Charles and Lady Diana _____ seven times.
3. Everybody knows that Bette Midler's _____ are not as large as Dolly Parton's.
4. If Gloria Steinem had her way, convicted rapists would have their _____ cut off.
5. Most people think Warren Beatty is a _____ maniac, but the truth is he doesn't _____ more than once a month.
6. Henry Kissinger loved to _____ all the Hollywood starlets he used to go out with before he was married.
7. Although Truman Capote frankly confesses to being one, Gore Vidal has never openly admitted he's a _____.
8. Brooke Shields still winces when she thinks of all the men leering at that nude baby picture of her in the bathtub with her _____ sticking out of the water.
9. Despite her libel suit victory over *The National Enquirer*, which called her a lush, Carol Burnett actually is a confirmed _____ who attends _____ meetings.
10. Nancy Reagan likes to have _____ with the President at least once a week.
11. While in the Navy during World War II, Don Rickles got a case of _____ from a Hawaiian girl.
12. It was a well-publicized fact that ex-President Jimmy Carter developed hemorrhoids in his _____.
13. Insiders agree that Milton Berle has the biggest _____ in Show Business.
14. Lenny Bruce was the first to admit on stage that eating beans made him _____ all night long.
15. Intimates swear that Robert Redford is a closet _____.

If you came up with any other answers than these, you've got an X-RATED mind! 1. baldness 2. danced 3. film grosses 4. paroles 5. health, exercise 6. impress 7. mystery story lover 8. rubber duck 9. parent, PTA 10. tea 11. champagne 12. term of office 13. ego 14. nauseous 15. re-arranger

WAR IS HELLER DEPT.

You loved the book, right? So you should fall over in ecstasy at the movie, right? Not so fast, speed-readers! Something happened, and no one is quite sure what it was. Let's just say that this one movie could single-handedly revive the lost art of reading. On the other hand, this MAD satire of the movie could very well kill it again. In any case, here is our version of—

Mumble mumble, mumble mumble mumble mumble mumble mumble mumble umble . . . mum-mumble mumble ble umble!

Mumble mumble mumble mumble mumble mumble mumble mumble mumble mumble mumble mum-ble mumble!

Why are we **talking** with these B-25's taking off?! Nobody can **HEAR** us!

Exactly! If they **COULD** hear us, they'd know this is the **END of the picture!**

But it's **NOT** the end! It's the **BEGINNING** of the picture!

Except that **this** picture begins with the end!

That's so people who **know** the beginning will think it's all **over**! And people who **don't** know the end will never know it **IS** the end until they see the **real** beginning all over **again** at the end! Understand, Shmoessarian?

I think so!

That means you don't

VROOM!

ATCH-ALL-22

ARTIST: MORT DRUCKER   WRITER: STAN HART

Okay, so I don't understand! There are **lots** of things in this picture I don't understand!

F'rinstance, this...!! ARRRGHH!! The picture isn't even three minutes old and already I'm **dead!**

Help him! Help the **Bombardier!**

I'm the Bombardier! I'm **okay!**

Are you **SURE** you're the Bombardier?

Of course I'm sure!

Then you're **NOT** the Bombardier! If you **SAY** you are, then you're **NOT!** You should have said you **WEREN'T** the Bombardier! Then you **WOULD** be! Understand...?

Can I have permission to bail out?

Of this plane?

No... of this **PICTURE!**

Doc, I gotta get out of **combat!** I want you to **ground** me!

I **can't**. In order to be grounded, you have to be **crazy!**

And anyone who **wants** to get out of combat obviously **isn't crazy!** That's the Army's "Catch-all—22"!

B*t*—don't you think I'm crazy?

Sure—for being in this **screwy** picture!

Good! Then get me out of this **screwy** picture!

I **can't**. In order to get out of a **picture**, you have to be **crazy!**

And anyone who **wants** to get out of a **screwy picture** obviously **isn't crazy!** That's HOLLYWOOD's "Catch-all—22"!

87

Panel 1:
- Hi, there, pilots! This is **Major Dandy**! You **WILL** be careful with your **planes** on today's mission... won't you? They cost **$2 million** to rent!
- After all, it's not **easy** to find thirty B-25's that can **still fly** twenty-five years after World War II!
- How come his face never moves when he talks?
- His **real-life WIFE** is in this picture!
- What's **THAT** got to do with it?
- She's a **ventriloquist**!

Panel 2:
- I GOTTA GET OUT OF HERE! I'M SICK! I'M SICK TO MY STOMACH!
- What's the **matter**, Shmoessarian? You sick from having to drop **bombs** on innocent women and children?
- No, I'm sick from having to smell that **disgusting pipe** of yours!

Panel 3:
- Except for **one little thing**, I have it all figured out! I swap the **parachutes** for a warehouse full of **Malomars**! Then, I swap the **Malomars** for ten carloads of **loose-leaf reinforcements**! Then... I swap **THEM**!
- What do you swap them for?
- I swap them for **parachutes**!
- What's the point of all that?
- That's the one little thing I haven't figured out yet!

Panel 4:
- That **crazy Wily Wheelerdealer** sold my parachute! Well— I don't **care**! I'm **STILL** gonna jump!
- No, Shmoessarian! You **can't** jump without a **parachute**! You'll be **KILLED**!
- If it gets me out of this screwy picture, death can't be **ALL** bad!

Panel 5:
- This must be one of my **fantasy** scenes! Tell me, what does my trying to swim to you while you stand there—stark naked—**symbolize**?
- It symbolizes about **$5 million EXTRA** at the **box office**! This ain't no old-fashioned **John Wayne War Movie**, y'know!
- Okay—but why am I **DROWNING**? Think of how much **MORE** it would symbolize if I could **REACH** you!

Panel 6:
- Hi, Shmoessarian! I understand that Col. Catheter has increased the number of missions from **50 to 75**!
- You've got to **help me**, Chaplain Tapdance! I don't want to **fly** any more! I've found a **reason** for **living**! There's something I have to **DO** before I die!
- What's that?
- Take **swimming lessons**!
- REMEMBER, DON'T FIDGET!

88

How come this scene is in the picture?
You mean, to surprise the audience?
For shock value!
No, to surprise HIM! He doesn't know the camera is going!
Tell me one thing, Nurse Ducky? Why in hell are you in this picture?
I'm Major Dandy's wife . . . in real life!
So?! I'm the STAR of the movie, and my wife's not in it!
She's not a ventriloquist!!
I'm General Draidle . . . and I've brought these people along to give you men an opportunity . . .
To do what, Sir?
. . . to do the "Horny G.I." bit! It's in every Army picture they ever made!
That's very kind of you, Sir!
It also gives me a chance to do the "Grumpy Big Man and his Dopey Son-In-Law" bit! You know the one! You've seen that in hundreds of movies, too!
Yes sir!
If there are any clichés we left out, call me!
Boy! Col. Catheter just raised the number of missions from 75 to 100!
Great!! Now, I won't have to go home!
Are you crazy?! Why don't you want to go home?
My folks will send me to Day Camp!
Hey! Did you hear that? Up to now, there hasn't been a note of background music!
Suddenly, SHE walks by and—TA-DAH!! What IS that theme, anyway! It—it sounds familiar!
That's the theme from "2001"!
What's THAT music doing in THIS picture?
Why argue with success?!

| Aren't you **out of uniform**, Shmoessarian? | **Everyone** walks around like this today! | In the **Army**?! | No, in the **movies**!! | This is **ridiculous**! I can't give this man a medal!! | Why **not**? | There's nothing to pin it on! |

| Let's make love... | Why **not**?! | What?! **Another** flashback?! **Nuts**!! Just when I was beginning to **enjoy** this role! | Help him! Help the **Bombardier**! | You **are**?! Then let me talk to the **Bombardier**! | Oh?! Please tell the **Bombardier** I called! | Sorry to **disturb** you! I was looking for the **Bombardier**! |
| Not so **fast**, Shmoessarian! | First, you have to have a **flashback**! | | **I'M** the Bombardier! I'm **okay**! | **I AM** the Bombardier! | But **I'M** the Bombardier! | I'll tell him when he comes in! | Hey! Don't **YOU** start! |

| Italy weel **lose** ze war, but eet weel be **victorious**! | Gee, old Italian man... you **really** confuse me! | Why? Because I speek een **paradoxes**?! | No, because you speak with a **French** accent! | Come-a, Nutly! Let's-a make-a love now... | I can't right now! Wait... | Until-a **when**?? | Until I reach **puberty**! |

90

Just pretend you're their dying son, Shmoessarian!
The audience won't know! If they don't think it's funny, then they'll think it was supposed to be funny! And if they think it IS funny! they'll never know it wasn't funny!
And this is supposed to be funny?!?
You mean . . .
Right! That's NICHOLS' "Catch-all—22"!
How come a very minor character like you seems to be in almost every scene?
I wrote the screenplay! I made sure that I was!
Boy, that's chutzpah!
Say one more nasty thing, and I'll LET him shoot you!
The script is better than the book! Much better! I love it! LOVE IT!!
All right, planes! Be careful not to hit our warehouses! Just men and hospitals!
Wily! You're INSANE!!
It's strictly a commercial arrangement, Shmoessarian!
I made a deal to get rid of those parachutes we've been stuck with! I swapped them for some bombs!
Okay, but did you have to arrange to have them DELIVERED?!
Bon giorno, Shmoessarian! Is-a my Nutly come-a soon?
The Germans?!
No . . . they got him!
No . . . the Truant Officers!!
EVERYTHING YOU ALWAYS WANTED TO KNOW ABOUT SEX*
D. REUBEN MD
THE SENSUAL WOMAN!
Hey!
Hey, this is terrific!
Whoopie! I finally got out of that screwy picture!
What makes you think so?
Don't you see all those disgusting, sordid things going on in these Rome streets? I'm in a FELLINI movie!

FIDDLER MADE A GOOF DEPT.

Practically everyone has seen the prize-winning musical about the loveable people in that little village in Old Russia called Anetevka. Well, as far as we're concerned, "Fiddler" made a GOOF! Because a show like that is very sentimental and touching until we think about the *descendents* of those oppressed people who fled Europe so many years ago, and how those descendents have almost destroyed a Dream. Which is why MAD now takes this famous musical about the problems of people who had *nothing,* and updates it with a version about the problems of people who have *everything* —mainly America's Upper Middle Class. Here, then, is our sing-along rendition, re-titled . . .

Antenna

ARTIST: MORT DRUCKER

An antenna on the roof! What's so strange about **that?** Nothing much . . . except that **this** antenna is on the roof of our **kennel!**

You see, here in our **$150,000** home in the suburbs, even our **dog** is spoiled rotten!

You may ask: Why do I work so hard to provide such luxuries as a **Zenith Color TV Console** for our dog? Why not just a simple **Black-and-White Emerson Portable?**

Because here in the **suburbs,** a family is measured by **one yardstick—POSSESSIONS!**

Possessions are what earn us the **respect** and **admiration** of the people who mean the **most** to us! And who are they . . . ? **THE NEIGHBORS!!**

Still, it's not so easy being prosperous! Even **WE** have our problems! And what are our **biggest** ones . . . ? **OUR DAUGHTERS!**

POSSESSIONS!   **THE NEIGHBORS!**   **OUR DAUGHTERS!**

on the Roof

WRITER: FRANK JACOBS

As a trained Psychiatrist, Mr. Buckchaser, I must tell you that this case is rather unusual!

Why?? Don't you believe in Group Therapy?

Yes, but for an entire family?!? Besides, I've never worked this way before—as a sleep-in Analyst!

Good! Just so we're the first on our block to have one! Now, shut up... and listen to our problems...

*****Head-shrinker, head-shrinker,
I'm a success—
Three-car garage—
Fancy address;
Head-shrinker, head-shrinker,
Look deep inside
And find out why I'm a mess!**

**Head-shrinker, head-shrinker,
I am his spouse—
Two minks I own—
One's for the house;
I'm just a typical,
Rich, pampered wife—
So why do I hate my life?**

*Sung to the tune of "Matchmaker, Matchmaker"

I'm Shei-la—A Free Sex fanatic!

I'm Nan-cy—A speed freak just now!

I'm Joy, who Makes bombs in the attic And answers the phone with Quotations from Mao!

**Head-shrinker, head-shrinker,
This is our fate—
Kids we can't stand!
Parents we hate!**

**Millions just like us
Throughout ev'ry state!
So—Don't fall asleep—
Make with the Freud—**

**Say something deep—
Give us a clue—
So all of us can
Hate you!**

93

The headshrinker said I treat my daughters like possessions, not like human beings! He's right! I'll start by making up with my daughter Sheila!

Hello, my darling dependent! To own you is to love you!

Bug off with the soft soap, Pop! I'm eloping with "Floyd And The Wheat Germs"!

You're marrying a Rock Group?

We don't want a big wedding! Just a quiet nude ceremony with a few dozen close porno freak friends in attendance!

Such a dilemma! My first born—running off to live with a bunch of strangers! On the other hand, she's been doing that HERE for 18 years! On the other hand, it's not like I'd be losing my Cadillac! On the other hand, do I really care??

We're free! Your father gave us his blessing!

If you think "Drop Dead!" is a blessing, you're flakier than I thought! Still, it gives us an excuse to go running naked through the woods, celebrating the wonders and miracles of today's counter-culture!

*Coolest of coolest—
Grooviest of grooviest—
Kids wearing love beads
Round their necks;
Making the scene till,
Grooviest of grooviest,
We give grown-ups tips on sex!

Coolest of coolest—
Grooviest of grooviest—
Stu-dents went marching in a rage;
Look how the land berated them, hated them,
Then reduced the voting age!

*Sung to the tune of "Miracle of Miracles"

When John told Yoko,
"Let's pose bare!"
That was the grooviest!
When thousands were freaked out
At the Woodstock Fair,
That was the grooviest, too!

But of all the grooviest
Scenes we've found,
By far the grooviest
One around
Is that we've been spoofing
This show so square
Till...it...now...looks...
More...like..."Hair"!

Tell me, Doc—what made Sheila run off with a Rock Group instead of marrying someone with a guaranteed income—like a Doctor, a Lawyer or a Railroad Brakeman??

Perhaps she disliked being treated as another one of your acquisitions!

Nonsense! We've loved her ever since we brought her home from the showroom!

94

Life is often **hard** here in the suburbs! Sometimes, I think I'd be **better** off if I were **worse** off!

*If I were a poor man—
Scuba duba duba
Duba duba duba duba dee;
All my hang-ups
Would be leaving me,
If I were a
Needy man!

Wouldn't have an ulcer—
Scuba duba duba
Duba duba duba duba dee;
I'd be living
Off so-ci-e-ty
If I were a
Needy man!

I'd...simp...ly...
Sign my name and draw "Unemployment"
Each week I didn't have a job;
And should the Welfare
Man doubt my word some-how—
I'd say I'd tried my best to find some employment
Then I would tell him with a sob:
"But no one seems to need a SHEPHERD now!"

*Sung to the tune of "If I Were a Rich Man"

I'd...wake...at
Noon and watch my new color TV,
Fresh from the leading local store,
For which I got for only five dollars down;
And...when...they
Took it back for missing the payments
I'd put five dollars down once more,
Until I'd gone through ev'ry store in town!

Ahhhhh!

If I were a poor man—
Scuba duba duba
Duba duba duba duba dee!
I would be a living char-i-ty
If I were a needy man;
Wouldn't know from Miltown—
Scuba duba duba
Duba duba duba duba dee;
I would not need psycho-therapy
If I were a needy man;

I'd...try...my
Luck each day at playing the Numbers,
Then I would play the Lott-er-y—
I'd put each dime and
Nickel and quarter in,
And...when...I'd
Find I'd missed by only one number,
Oh, such excitement you would see—
But—
God forbid that I should ever win!

LOTTERY 50¢ TICKETS

I'd...see...my
Wife, that nagging bag of a spendthrift,
Charg-ing her clothes in great amounts
In dress stores in that
Big fancy shopping mall;
And when the stores found out that
She was a deadbeat,
Soon she would have no charge accounts—
And that would be the sweetest thing of all!

Ahhhhh!

If I were a poor man,
Scuba duba duba
Duba duba duba duba dee—
Junk mail lists would
Soon be dropping me
If I were a
Needy man;

Wouldn't know from "Status"—
Scuba duba duba
Duba duba duba duba dee;
Tax collectors would not audit me;
I would have no tax to pay, you see;
I would even drive a used Capri—
If I were a
Nee-dy
Man!

Still—I've got two daughters left! Look at my **Nancy!** The first girl in the neighborhood to play **"Doctor"** with **real hypodermics!**

Hi, Pop! You're just in time to say **goodbye!** I'm leaving for good with **Harvey The Head** here!

C'mon, Harvey! We're splitting for the **big city** while we sing this song that glorifies our holy quest for **a new spiritual experience!**

*Dope-pusher, dope-pusher,
Fix me a fix;
Push me a push!
Fill me with kicks;
Dope-pusher, dope-pusher,
Make with the score
And open your bag of tricks!

Dope-pusher, dope-pusher,
Sell me no grass;
It's now become
Too middle-class;
Zap me for good 'cause I'm
Counting on you
To hook me on something new!

*Reprise to the tune of "Matchmaker, Matchmaker"

Don't hype me
With second-hand acid;
Don't fake me
And say that I'll flip;
Don't goof me
With downs—they're too placid;
I'm looking right now
For the ultimate trip!

Dope-pusher, dope-pusher,
Hand us no hash;
We've got the bread;
You've got the stash;
Sooner or later
We're certain to crash,
So . . .

Speed us no speed;
Smack us no smack;
Weed us no weed;
Reach in the sky
And find us
The
High-est
High!

Such a **dilemma!** My daughter the junkie leaving **home!** On the **other** hand, she once pawned my **Omega** for a fix! On the **other** hand, she might **die** in the jungle out there! On the **other** hand, I've got her **life** insured for **two hundred grand!** On the **other** hand, she's usually so **stoned**, they won't be able to tell whether she's alive or dead **anyhow!**

WHAM!

Our children are **leaving** us, dear!

Yes! Now we can enter our **golden years** when we will sit quietly by ourselves and **grow old together!**

Grow OLD?!? Not if **you** can help it!

*Look at this woman
Pushing fif-ty—
Trying so hard
To hide the truth;
Now that she's getting
So much old-er—
She . . . seeks . . . youth;

Look at her going
To beaut-i-cians—
Giving her frame
An over-haul;
What treatment's
Left for her? She's
Had . . . them . . . all:

Hair dyed, hair set;
Old age? Not yet;
Wrinkles dis-appear—
One face-lift
Following another,
Tak-ing off
Still another year;

*Sung to the tune of "Sunrise, Sunset"

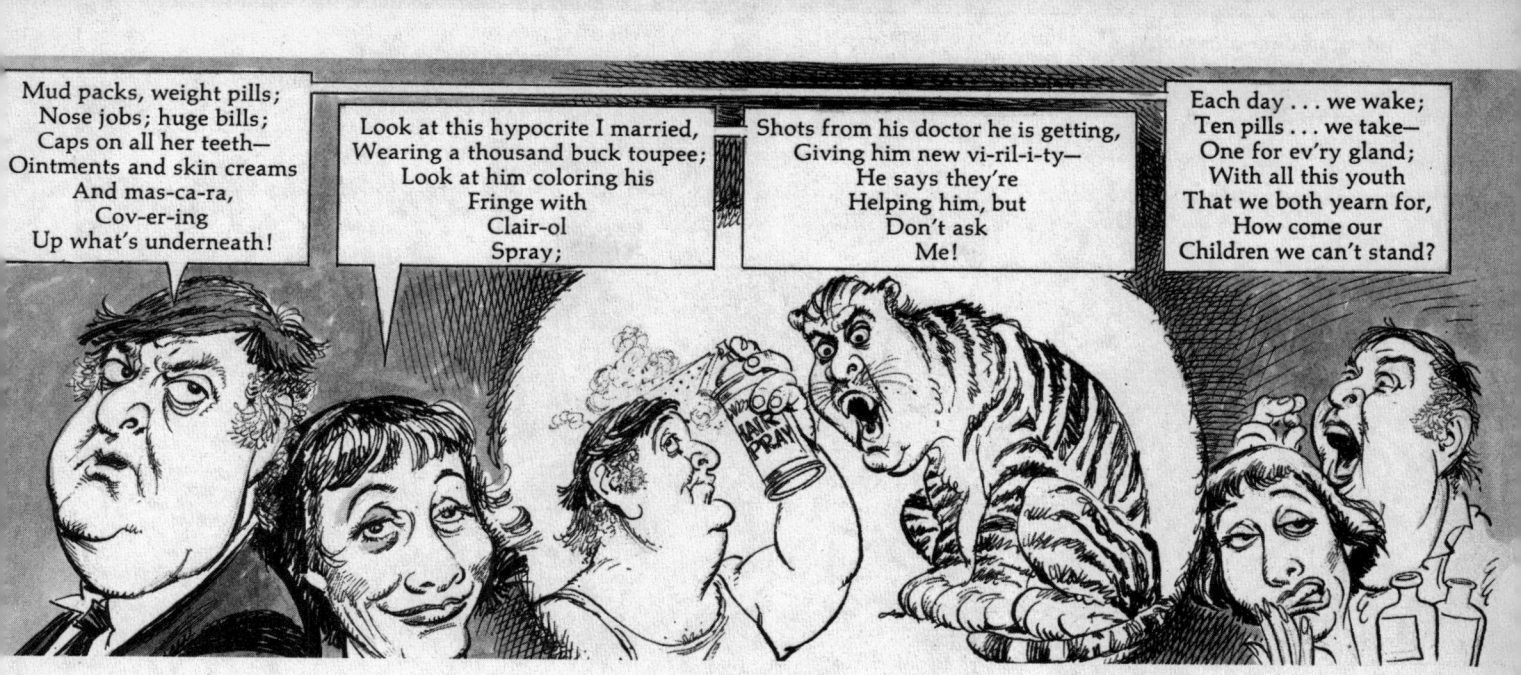

Mud packs, weight pills;
Nose jobs; huge bills;
Caps on all her teeth—
Ointments and skin creams
And mas-ca-ra,
Cov-er-ing
Up what's underneath!

Look at this hypocrite I married,
Wearing a thousand buck toupee;
Look at him coloring his
Fringe with
Clair-ol
Spray;

Shots from his doctor he is getting,
Giving him new vi-ril-i-ty—
He says they're
Helping him, but
Don't ask
Me!

Each day ... we wake;
Ten pills ... we take—
One for ev'ry gland;
With all this youth
That we both yearn for,
How come our
Children we can't stand?

Still—I've got my **youngest** daughter, my little **princess**, my **Joy!** Each day, she sits in her room, making **Molotov cocktails** out of my wife's empty **Geritol** bottles!

S'long, Pop! I'm gonna blow this nothing scene!

But, **why?** Haven't I given you everything you **wanted?** Didn't I bring the **Chicago Seven** to your **Sweet Sixteen Party?** Say you'll stay and I'll buy you your own very own **munitions plant!**

I'm **off** the **violence** kick, Pop! I'm into **Gay Liberation**, now! That's why I'm eloping with **Pauline** here!

Such a **dilemma!** My **daughter**, marrying a **GIRL!** On the **other** hand, she might be marrying a **Black!** On the **other** hand, I don't have to worry about her getting **pregnant!** On the **other** hand, I think it's time to talk to the **Analyst** again ...

So you see, Doctor ... they've all left us! Why? **WHY??**

For **that** answer, I need to probe your **subconscious!** Have you had any **unusual dreams** or **nightmares** lately?

Just **one!** I was sleeping the other night, when suddenly ...

Aaagh! No! Not YOU!!

What **is** it? Who—who's here in our **bedroom?!?**

It's—it's **THEM!** It's our **ancestors** from the **Old Country!** There's my Grandfather, **Tevya** ... and my Grandmother, **Golde** ... and **Motel**, the Tailor ... and **Yente**, the Matchmaker ... and **Lazar**, the Butcher ... and all the **other** people from **Anetevka!**

That's **right!** Back in Russia, we may not have had **Analysts**, but we could always recognize a **fool** when we saw one!

*Dum-dum of dum-dums!
Imbecile of Imbeciles!
God led us to the U.S.A.!
Said, "You are free," and,
Imbecile of imbeciles,
Look at what we find today!

Dum-dum of dum-dums!
Imbecile of Imbeciles!
God made a modern Cam-e-lot;
Now that we've seen the
Mess you've made,
We're afraid
God wants back his melting pot!

When Yippies tear the flag to shreds—
They act like imbeciles;
When hard-hats go crazy and start busting heads—
They act like imbeciles, too;

But though God's seen imbeciles great and small,
The most incredible thing of all
Is that God might as well say he is through—
None...will...e-ver...e-qual...you!

Dum-dum of dum-dums!
Imbecile of imbeciles!
Long years we suffered by the score;
Then we looked *here*, you
Imbecile of imbeciles;
Now...we...suf-fer...e-ven...more!

When in-dus-tries pollute the land,
They act like imbeciles;
When un-ions keep striking till they're out of hand,
They act like imbeciles, too;

But though God's made imbeciles great and small,
The thing that bothers us most of all
Is that we fear that God may make a fuss
And...some...how...blame...you...on...us!

*Reprise to the tune of "Miracle of Miracles"

No. 176

MAD

IN THIS ISSUE, WE SOCK "AIRPORT '75"!

INSIDE DOPE DEPT.

There's a great movie playing around. It's exciting, and full of action, and it's easy to watch. It's not one of those movies where you have to think! Or is it?? You certainly don't do any thinking during the movie. But after it's over, you're left with a couple of unanswered questions. In fact, *everybody* is left with a couple of unanswered questions. Take f'rinstance the guy who gets shot in the very first scenes:

Okay! So I walked around Marseilles! So this brown Mark III Lincoln Continental followed me! So I bought a French bread, and I bought a pizza, and I stepped into this doorway, and now I'm being—**GAAAK!**—murdered! So after the picture is all over, maybe somebody will tell me . . .

BLAM BLAM

Hey, kid, tell me! Do you believe in Santa Claus?

Well, I used to . . . until you started showing up around here—in JULY!!

An' I never saw Santa wearing a gun before! I think you're a cop!!

Well, I'm **NOT**, you little brat! And if you say that one more time, I'm gonna arrest you!

I'll have a Frank with sauerkraut . . . and a bottle of Pepsi!

I don't **have** any Franks . . . sauerkraut . . . **OR** bottles of Pepsi!

Then what's in the cart?

DISGUISES!! Now . . . beat it!!

WHAT'S THE CONNECTION?

ARTIST: MORT DRUCKER   WRITER: DICK DE BARTOLO

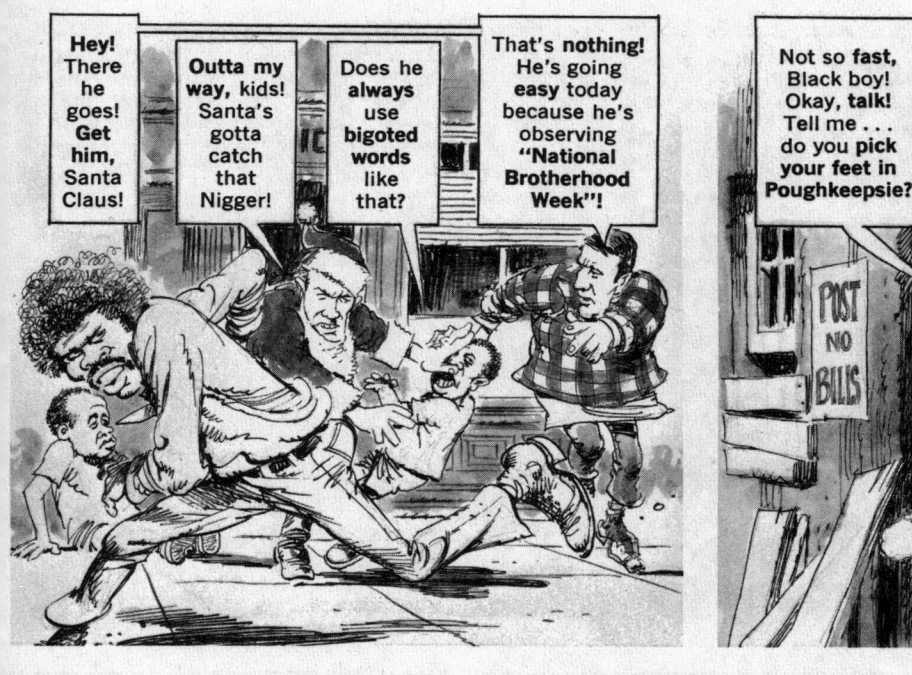

Panel 1:
- Hey! There he goes! **Get** him, Santa Claus!
- **Outta** my way, kids! Santa's gotta catch that Nigger!
- Does he always use bigoted words like that?
- That's **nothing**! He's going easy today because he's observing "National Brotherhood Week"!

Panel 2:
- Not so **fast**, Black boy! Okay, **talk**! Tell me... do you pick your feet in Poughkeepsie?
- Huh? Man, I thought some of **US** talked funny... but you **is** weird!!
- Listen, punk! I'm not letting you go till you **answer** me! DO YOU PICK YOUR FEET IN POUGHKEEPSIE?
- No, but I pick my nose in Harlem!

Panel 3:
- Close enough! Now, **talk**! Who's giving you the stuff? Bill the Barber? Sam the Shoemaker? Pete the Podiatrist?
- **Talk**, punk! You know, I can put you away for a long long time! You **believe** that, **don't** you, punk??
- I believe! I believe!
- Look! Isn't it wonderful to see that some of the **bigger** kids **still** believe in Santa Claus?!

Panel 4:
- C'mon, Cockeye! You've hit him enough! You're hurting your **fist**! Let's put him in the **car** and drive him **downtown**...
- Okay! But in **THAT** case, let me give him **one more** for the road!
- You know what your **problem** is, Cockeye? By the time you get through **working** over a wanted man, he never matches his **description**, and we gotta let him **go**!

101

Hey, Birdie! Did you see? That guy gave the waiter a $100 tip!
Well? What's so unusual about that?
It's not even his waiter! And now he's giving the hat check girl a $50 tip!
Well? What's so unusual about that?
He doesn't even have a hat! There's something fishy going on here! That kind of tipping makes me suspicious! And the fact that they're all wearing GUNS doesn't help! C'mon! Let's follow 'em!
Cockeye, the last time we followed someone, we stayed up for 3 days and 3 nights, went 48 hours without food, and accidentally killed a Federal Agent!
Well . . . I can't promise it will be as much fun as THAT—but let's give it a whirl!
Gee, Cockeye, you're doing a great job of staying right on their tail!
No problem, Birdie! I tied our bumpers together!
But don't you think they'll get a little suspicious—seeing the same car behind them five hours in a row—especially in deserted Brooklyn?!?
Naw! I keep changing my expression and they think I'm someone different each time they look!
Hey! The guy drives a Caddy, his girl is loaded down with expensive clothes and jewelry, and they come home to a dumpy little Candy Store like that! What do you think, Cockeye?
I think that Candy Store is a GOLD MINE! We should open one right across the street and steal his customers!
CIGARS
SNUFF
DUMPY
CANDY
STORE
BAR
JOE'S
BARBER SHOP
I'm going to New York!
I bought you a new camera!
I bought you a new coat!
That's great! Now tell me, what's the connection?
I got the scoop on those Candy Store sweeties! His name is Salvatore Giuseppe Bocciballo, and his wife's name is Angelina Bocciballo!
Oh, they're Italians?
No, Wops!
Wasn't this a great idea of mine? I figured Bocciballo was getting a little suspicious of seeing a car behind him all the time, so I came up with this . . .
Yeah, but don't you think that sitting in his BACK SEAT is a little dangerous?
Not so loud! He'll hear you! Now this is what I found out so far! Bocciballo and his wife make about $7000 a year from the Candy Store . . . and they spend $80,000!
Boy, I wish MY wife could stretch a buck like that!

Hey, we're stopping at Sol Beanstalk's apartment! I've been wanting to get something on him for years!
Yeah! They say he's a big bank-roller of illicit narcotics!
Who cares about that!? He's Jewish! That's what galls me! I don't know why those Jews don't go back to Jewland where they came from!
You know, Cockeye! Sometimes you sound like a bigot!
Listen, I don't have any love for them Bigots, either! If I had my way, every one of THEM would be sent back to Bigotland where THEY came from!
And what is the purpose of your visit to America, Mr. Dapperbeaux?
I have come from France to drive my custom-built Mark III Lincoln Continental into Brooklyn where I will park it in the worst run-down section of the waterfront!
Yes, but what's the connection??
Gee, I was hoping YOU guys would know?
SMACK
Okay, this is a raid! I want all the goodies on the counter!
Gee, Cockeye, why can't you come through the front door just once! This is the fourth plate glass window you've busted this month!
Boy, there are more pills, needles and drugs on that counter than in the last place Cockeye busted!!
Where was that?
The Upjohn Pharmaceutical Company!
UPS
Hey, Spade! Haven't seen you in a Coon's age! How's my little Black-Eyed Pea?
You talkin' to me?
Don't get cute with me, Sambo, or I might start some name-calling!
Hey, Man! You got a dime to lend me for the John . . .?
Wait, I'll open it for you!
PAY NOW GO LATER
Okay! (SOCK!) No one can hear us now! (PUNCH!) So what's the word?
There's a big shipment due!
When? (SLAM!)
Soon! Maybe this week!
How much? (CRACK!)
I dunno! (OOOF!) A lot!
Now I'm gonna knock you back outside with one last shot! Thanks for the info! You're really a friend . . .
Thank God I'm a FRIEND! I'd hate to see the way he treats his ENEMIES!

But, Lieutenant Simpleton! I'm **sure** I'm on to something **BIG!!**
Cockeye, the last **time** you were on to something big, you cost the Department **$40,000, 2 police cars and one Federal Agent . . . !**
Yeah, but last time, I just had a **"feeling"!** This time, I got a **real "HUNCH"!**
Oh, well, if you're **THAT** positive, I'll assign a **Fed** to help! Let's see, who won't I **miss** if he gets **shot** accidentally??
OUR LEADER
What kind of a place **is this, anyway?**
It's an **Auto Graveyard . . .** where they auction off **old cars!**
See that guy in the **black hat?** He's our **agent!** He's bidding on a **beat-up wreck** of an **old car** for us!
Great! Now, can I ask just **one more question?**
WHAT'S THE CONNECTION???
Why'd we stop in this restaurant for a twelve course dinner? It makes **no sense at all!** The food is **lousy** here!
It's not for the **food!** It's for the **fantastic view!**
This is our **best table,** Sir . . . overlooking **Irving's TV Repair Shop,** where you can eat your dinner in **warmth** and **comfort** while you watch that **Narco agent** watch **you!**
IRVING'S TV REPAIR SHOP
PIZZA
MENU
Here! I got you some **Pizza!**
Guinea food again? I'd love some **Chink food** for a change!
Excuse me, Sir! I just want to tell you that you're doing a **real great job!**
You mean tracking down the **narcotics shipment?**
No, **insulting Minority Groups!** You're a real credit to all the Micks!
TUFF
STUFF
LECITHIN
Okay! Okay! I'm **waiting!** Is the stuff **good?**
Yeah, Man! It's like **great!**
Oh, **wow!** Who was **killed?** Cockeye? Birdie? **Someone vital to the plot!**
Naw! **Nobody!** It's just that there's been no **violence** for nearly **90 seconds,** so we just **stuck in** this plain old **bloody, gory, disgusting car wreck!**
(CHOKE!) Yeah, but what's the **connection?**
NY PD
LONG ISLAND EXPRESSWAY EASTBOUND
RIGHT LANE MUST TURN LEFT
NORTH
495

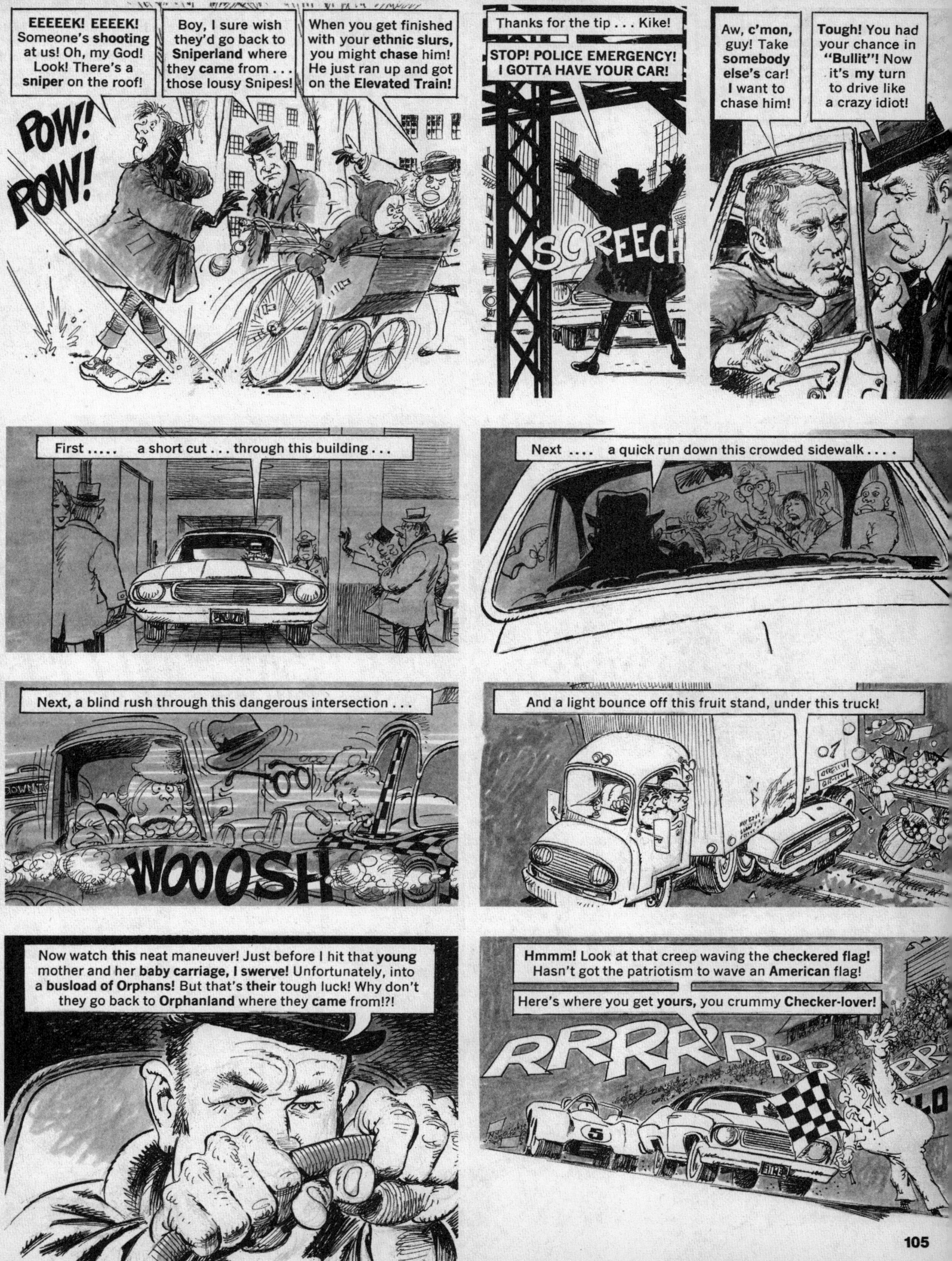
EEEEEK! EEEEK! Someone's shooting at us! Oh, my God! Look! There's a sniper on the roof!
POW! POW!
Boy, I sure wish they'd go back to Sniperland where they came from . . . those lousy Snipes!
When you get finished with your ethnic slurs, you might chase him! He just ran up and got on the Elevated Train!
Thanks for the tip . . . Kike!
STOP! POLICE EMERGENCY! I GOTTA HAVE YOUR CAR!
SCREECH
Aw, c'mon, guy! Take somebody else's car! I want to chase him!
Tough! You had your chance in "Bullit"! Now it's my turn to drive like a crazy idiot!
First ..... a short cut . . . through this building . . .
Next .... a quick run down this crowded sidewalk . . . .
Next, a blind rush through this dangerous intersection . . .
WOOOSH
And a light bounce off this fruit stand, under this truck!
Now watch this neat maneuver! Just before I hit that young mother and her baby carriage, I swerve! Unfortunately, into a busload of Orphans! But that's their tough luck! Why don't they go back to Orphanland where they came from!?!
Hmmm! Look at that creep waving the checkered flag! Hasn't got the patriotism to wave an American flag!
Here's where you get yours, you crummy Checker-lover!
RRRRRRRR

C'mon, buddy! Put down the gun, will you! These poor people have been held up six times already . . . and we've only gone two stops!!
Don't stop at any station or I'll shoot!
Actually, I hadn't planned to! What do those dumb New Yorkers expect for 35¢ anyway?!? Scheduled stops?!!
LOCAL
What's going on???
Probably a cop after a wanted criminal!
I sure hope he catches him fast! So far, he's killed 245 innocent law-abiding-citizen bystanders!!
How'd you like that for exciting driving, eh? I sure got here before the train . . . didn't I??
You sure did! The last train station is two miles back!!
DONT WALK
Take that, you lousy Snipe!
Now you know what it feels like to be shot to death!
Maybe next time, you won't be so quick to try to kill somebody!
BLAM!
POLISH EMBISSY JOKE DEPT
Okay, so we sit here all night staking out the Mark III Lincoln that Dapperbeaux brought from France! So tell me . . . what's the connection?
Search me?!? But here come a gang of Spics looking to strip it! Isn't that GREAT?!?
What's so great?! It spoils the stake-out!
Yeah, but it gives us a chance to hit Spics! We haven't hit Spics once so far !
#$%¢ Spics! Why don't they go back to Spicland where they came from!?!
But you're right! The stake-out is ruined! Take the car to the station and search it, and arrest the Spics!
On what charge . . . ?
Noodling their navels in Nantucket!
Is that a crime?
It carries twice the penalty of diddling your digit in Dallas!

Panel 1:
- Listen, Cockeye—
- Fed, I've had it up to **here** with you **razzin'** me!!
- But all I said was "Listen, Cockeye—"
- Yeah, but if I let you get away with **that**, the next thing you know you'll be making it into a **sentence**! You've been on my back ever since I accidentally killed your **best friend**! Can't you **forget** a petty grudge?

Panel 2:
- Didn't find a thing, Cockeye! We checked the roof, the floor, the engine, the tires, the seats ... **everything**!
- Did you look in the **trunk**?
- The trunk?!? **No**! What a **fantastic idea**! Hey, Gus! Look in the **trunk**!
- Cockeye's right! The stuff is **here** ...!
- Boy, you dumb Mechanics oughta all go back to **Mechanicland** where you **came** from! Now put the car **back together again**! Dapperbeaux's **waiting** for it!

Panel 3:
- Here you are, Mr. Dapperbeaux ... in **perfect shape**!
- Wait a minute! What's going on here, anyway?
- No matter what you **say**, Dapperbeaux, we never **searched** your car!
- Who said anything about **searching** my car!? I lost a **brown Lincoln Continental** and you're giving me back a **green Cadillac Eldorado**!
- **Phew!** is that all?! For a minute, we thought you were **suspicious**!

Panel 4:
- Well, **you've** got your **heroin** ... and **I've** got my **money**! Outside of a few million **loopholes**, it was the **perfect crime**!
- HOLD IT! THIS IS THE POLICE!

Panel 5:
- Sorry, guys, but this **isn't** the perfect crime! And we still have **three more loopholes** to create!
- I'm going to run and **hide** on this tiny, escape-proof island, and **never be found** by any of the **200 cops** you have here! That's loophole #1!
- And I'm going to get myself into a place where I can be **accidentally shot** by Cockeye! That's loophole #2!
- And many of the hoods involved in this crime who came to this island and shot it out with the police will be released for "**insufficient evidence**"! I thought shooting at a cop would at **least** be a **misdemeanor**! And that's loophole #3!

Panel 6:
- Well, anyway, on behalf of the American people, we want to thank you, Cockeye, for pursuing these criminals to the end!
- Well, I appreciate the compliment, but it **wasn't** me alone! No, sir, it was a **combination** of guys ... a regular potpourri of Dagos, Hebes, Fags, Spades, Polacks, Krauts ...
- Yeah, but what's the **connection**??

VIDIOT'S DELIGHT DEPT.

Recently, an author came up with what he thought was a brilliant idea: Namely, to write a novel about how a simple-minded idiot becomes the respected advisor to those at the highest level of power. But what he seems to have forgotten is that simple-minded idiots have been in charge around here for at least 2000 years, and maybe a lot longer! Oh, well, why quibble? In any case, they've made a movie based on his book, so let's see what happens when a modern moron finds out how far he can go in this world of ours just by

Bein

g NOT ALL There

A TV in the garden, TOO?! How'd THAT get here?!

I planted it, Luwheeze! See how nice it's growing?? It was only a little SONY last Spring!

Trance, you ARE bananas! You can't plant television sets like flowers! You ... sniff— sniff—Wait a minute! What's that awful smell?!? Is that really MANURE on that TV set?

No, Luwheeze! It's Chuck Barris!

Maybe this can penetrate that cabbage which you laughingly call a head! Our employer— Mr. Lemming— is DEAD!

I don't understand ...

Maybe I can explain it in your terms, Trance! Remember that terrible tragedy last week ... when you were watching "Captain Kangaroo" ... ?

Oh, NO! Poor Mr. Lemming blew a TUBE?!

Not just A tube!

You mean—?

That's right! His MAIN PICTURE tube!

ARTIST: MORT DRUCKER   WRITER: LARRY SIEGEL

Oh! NOW, I understand!! Put him down! Believe me ... it won't do any good to bring him in to the shop!!

Look, there's no more work for a Housekeeper and a Gardener here, Trance! I'm going to get a job somewhere else! What about YOU?

I think I'll just stay here and watch TV! And then maybe I'll donate my brain to Science!

Good idea! When you're READY, there's a thimble in my Sewing Kit!

Sir, we are the Lawyers for the Estate, and I'm afraid you're going to have to leave here!

Leave here?!? But I—I've never been outside this house before!! I—I can't take care of myself, and I only have an IQ of 27! What am I going to DO?!?

Well, have you ever thought about running for CONGRESS?!

109

Can anyone really be THAT stupid and tuned-out?!
I think it's a big put-on! Washington's a rough town, but once he gets to know the place, he'll be okay!
I'm not so sure!
Why not?
Well, for starters, he just asked me how to get to Sesame Street!
GET WHITEY
FRANK
AL
FREE THE FLN
GOD BLESS AMERICA
SPEED KILLS
It's so strange being away from the house!
Excuse me, Madam . . . I'm very tired and hungry . . . !
Would you mind feeding me . . . bathing me . . . and tucking me into bed . . . ?
WHAT?!? Are you CRAZY?!
Well, if you're going to make a Federal case out of it, forget it! Just CHANGE ME, and I'll be on my way . . . !
What a funny woman! I asked her to change me, and she went to sleep right on the sidewalk!
CHANGE you? Hey . . . you talkin' about DIAPERS, White Man?
Heh, heh, heh! Oh no, silly! WHY would I wear diapers?
Well, thank the Lord . . .
I always use PAMPERS! They stay TWICE as dry . . . and they're MUCH GENTLER on my tender . . .
SOUL FOOD
BAG
Another one! My goodness . . . people go to sleep so EARLY around here!
Oh, look! Here comes a group of nice young men! Perhaps THEY can help me . . .
Pardon me, Gentlemen . . . but is this Sesame Street?
No, Whitey! It's MY street! And the letter for today is "H" . . . !
Alfred E. Neuman for President
Like in "help" and "humanity"?
Like in "hate" and "honky"!
YOU'RE not the BIG BIRD!!
No, but you're a DEAD TURKEY!
My-my! Everybody is so excitable around here . . . !
HEY . . . WATCH IT . . . !
KLONK

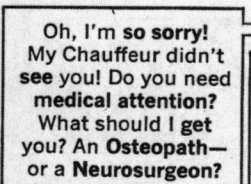

Panel 1:
- Oh, I'm so sorry! My Chauffeur didn't see you! Do you need medical attention? What should I get you? An Osteopath—or a Neurosurgeon?
- Whichever one kisses booboos and makes them ALLLLLLL better!
- Good Lord! He's—He's delirious! I'd better take him home with me...!

Panel 2:
- My name is Heave Grand! I'm the Wife of one of the most powerful business tycoons in America! I'm a very rich woman!
- My name is Trance! I'm a moron...!
- You're a WHAT?!?
- You have a very nice TV set here in your car, Heave! Gee, I sure miss Donny and Marie on the tube! They're MY kind of PEOPLE...!
- Oh, a MORMON!! My Husband and I are Episcopalians!

Panel 3:
- What a lovely house you have! And what a fine garden! I would like to work here... and plant radishes and tomatoes and cucumbers and lima beans! But above all...
- Now, we'll come to some kind of cash settlement for the accident! You're not going to be unreasonable, are you?
- ...I'll want lots and lots of lettuce!
- My God, he's going to bleed us DRY!!

Panel 4:
- I'm Dr. Allenbuzz! Now, don't worry! We're going to have you up and around in no time! Meanwhile, I'd better contact your own Physician! You DO see a Doctor regularly, don't you?
- Oh, yes! Trapper John, M.D.! He's very very good!
- Never heard of him! G.P.??
- NO, CBS!

Panel 5:
- Well, Trance, I've given you an exhaustive physical examination, and I've put you through a battery of laboratory tests! I now have the final results...
- Give it to me straight, Doctor! I can take it! What have I got?
- A severe case of DIAPER RASH!!
- I TOLD that woman to change me!

Panel 6:
- Trance, this is my wealthy and powerful Husband, Bane Grand! He's 80 years old, and he's dying!
- Gee... I'm terribly sorry to hear that! How long has he been in this condition?
- Ever since our Wedding Night... LAST WEEK!!
- The happiest three minutes of my life!

What a delicious dinner! Thank you both so much! And now, if you'll excuse me, I have to do something I always do after a meal! If someone will just . . .
Yes, of course! It's the third door on the left down the hall! You know something, Trance! I like you! You have the air of a Man in Command, a Captain of Industry! And yet, at the same time . . .
BELLLCCH!
Thank you for burping me, Jeeves!
. . . you seem to have that knack of knowing how to get close to the Working Class!
The President is coming to see me tomorrow! He often seeks my advice! I'd like you to join us and share some of your valuable thinking with him! What do you say?
Oh, yes, Bane! I would love to talk to the President about "The Jeffersons"!
Great! Tom was always one of his favorite Presidents!
. . . and "The Odd Couple"!
He always liked Dick and Pat Nixon, too! I have a feeling you'll go a long way here in Washington!
Secret Service! Sorry to bother you, but we're checking the house before the President arrives! What do you do here?
I watch television all the time, day and night! I'm watching one of my favorite shows now . . . !
I hate to bring this up, Sir—but you're looking at a Washing Machine!!
Hmmmmm! I kinda THOUGHT the screen was too small!
That's all right, Sir! We all make mistakes! I just got a message! Mr. Grand and the President are waiting for you in the den . . .
Tell them I'll be in, right after they break for the Rinse Cycle!
Mr. President . . . this is my newest and best friend, Trance! He has some interesting thoughts about those upcoming ELECTIONS! To him, the nation is like a garden!
Oh, yes, I know all about gardens! A garden has its seasons! First, there is Spring, then Summer, then Fall, then Winter! In the Spring, we plant a garden, In the Summer, it grows! In the Fall, it withers and in the Winter, it dies!
Brilliant!! What he is saying is: If you can't get Congress to pass laws in the Spring, the garden—the nation—will not grow over the Summer . . . and by Fall elections, it will be too late!

I'm not arguing with the fact that the country can be compared with a garden . . . but between you and me, what your friend just said was a crock of HORSE#$%&!
Of course!! What do you THINK makes a garden GROW . . . ?!?
By God, I never THOUGHT of THAT! He IS a genius!!
Hello, Mr. Trance! This is Freddie Silverman, the head of NBC! The President used your analogy about gardens last night, and the country absolutely loved it! Would you consider doing a "guest spot" on an NBC show . . . ??
Oh, thank you, Freddie, but I really have very little to say! I'm just a moron with an IQ of 27 . . . !!
A MORON?! With an IQ of 27?! That changes EVERYTHING!!
Would you consider STARRING in an NBC show?!
WE'RE NO. 3 AND WE'RE VERY TRYING.
And now . . . heeeeeeer's Trancey . . .
SCREAMS!
CLAP! CLAP!
Hello, America! A garden has its seasons! First, there is Fall, then Winter, then Spring and then Summer! In the Fall, the garden withers! In the Winter, it dies! In the Spring, we plant it again!
Brilliant! What he's saying is: If you plant a TV show and it withers in the Fall, you can replant it in the Spring!
He's done something amazing!
Right! He's just explained "The Second Season"!
Who IS he?!? Hasn't the FBI found anything about his background?
All they know is: he's an orphan, and he's been watching TV non-stop for 34 years! Oh, they did locate records dating back to 1948, listing some people as his closest relatives!
Ah-HAH!!! Now, we're getting somewhere! Who ARE they . . . ?
Kukla, Fran and Ollie!!
Now, folks—just follow this simple exercise . . .
Oh, yes, Mr. La Lanne, I always do EVERYTHING the TV set tells me to do!
KNOCK KNOCK KNOCK
Trance . . . it's me, Heave . . . ! Could I come in for a minute?
CLICK
. . . but you can call ME Suzy Chapstick!
You've become such a great man, Trance! The country needs you, the world needs you, and I need you!
Oh, darling! You want me to kiss you, don't you?!? I've waited so long for you to make love to me . . .
CLICK!

Mmmm! Mmmmm! Kentucky Fried Chicken is finger lickin' good . . .
Oh, God . . . I've never known such excitement! How did you KNOW my elbow is my wildest erogenous zone?!?
CLICK!
Thanks! I needed that . . . !
YOU'RE into S-M, TOO?! I can't believe it! Boy, are we going to have FUN!
SLAP SLAP SLAP!
CLICK!
Another fine mess you've gotten me into, Stanley!
Oh, darling, you really know how to make a woman FEEL like a woman! More! More . . . ! Hit me again!!
SPLAT!
This is terrible, Trance! My husband watched us making that wild, passionate love last night through a secret mirror in the next room . . . and he WENT—just like that!
He died from a heart attack?
No . . . they say he died LAUGH-ING!
SNAP
Trance, now that Bane Grand is gone and you've taken over his Wife and his fortune, I'm relying on you for important national decisions! Everyone agrees that you're the wisest man in the nation today!
Oh, thank you, Mr. President! I'd be very happy to help you!
Good! Now, here's where we stand! Those damned Russians are acting up in the Middle East and Southeast Asia! What PREPARATION do we make to finally STOP them?
So remember! To help shrink the swelling of painful hemorrhoidal tissues, use "Preparation H"!!
Yes! Use "Preparation H"!
Did you hear what Trance said?! "H"!! He wants us to use the "H"!!
The "H-Bomb"?! But, Mr. President! Do you realize what that MEANS?!
RATION H
Of course I do! But are YOU going to argue with the wisest man in the country . . . and maybe in the whole . . . cough! . . . gasp! . . . world?! ARRRRRGH! . . . PLOTZ!
BLAM! BLAST!
BOOM!
VOOM!

Drawing continuity

Continuity, such as a movie satire in *Mad Magazine* or an animated commercial of a celebrity, presents some of the most difficult problems in caricature. The artist cannot create one definitive study, as in a caricature that might appear with accompanying text or on a magazine cover. Rather, he must capture the likeness in panel one; then again in panel two in a different angle, pose, and composition; then again in panel three, and so on for as many as six or seven panels per page for perhaps six or seven pages. Drucker will often include a distant shot, a silhouette, or some other change of pace to allow both the reader and himself a rest.

"To keep the character looking like the same person throughout," suggests Drucker, "I study how the dominant features react in key expressions. If the lip curls in a particular way, or the eyes narrow more than usual while smiling, I can construct the head in various poses and still maintain a consistency in the likenesses despite little or no research in these new poses. It's always surprising to see how many photographs of people don't actually look like them. In a collection of movie stills from any one film you're sure to find several shots of an individual whom had you not known who it was you wouldn't be able to recognize. If I draw my characters that way—staying completely true to the reference material—it would be thought a bad job. That's why I try not to depend solely upon photos. Being an accurate copier doesn't ensure good likenesses. A caricaturist, like a portrait artist, deals not with reality, but with images reduced to line and/or tone on a two-dimensional surface."

Mort Drucker does something else, too. He adds an appealing quality, a style, that brings his two-dimensional surfaces to life. He's a warm, sensitive man whose caricatures are created to delight, not offend. Mix this with his remarkable talent and you have a recipe for success.

EATING OUT DEPT.

The latest hit movie making the rounds is about a creature from another planet. It's supposed to be an original film, but it's a lot like an old movie called "The Thing," and a little like "The Exorcist," with a touch of "Star Wars," and a hint of "The Creature From The Black Lagoon," with a slight echo of "Lost in Space." As a matter of fact, it reminds us of so many movies, instead of "Alien," it should be called...

- How long were we in the "Sleep Pods" this time?
- Four weeks! Boy... talk about sleeping through the alarm clock...!
- I keep forgetting that we sleep for weeks at a time! I think I'm gonna have to give up shaving BEFORE I go to bed!!
- You say we were asleep four weeks?!? Now I don't feel so bad about wetting the bed!!
- Frett and I talked it over... and we've decided we want an equal share of pay! After all, we LOADED this space tug!
- That's a big deal! This space tug has "AUTOMATIC LOAD!"
- Yeah, but WE were the ones who PUSHED the BUTTON!!
- Ho-hum! So much for THIS wake-up period's exciting and interesting conversation! This time, I suggest we go back to sleep for FIVE weeks!!

ALIAS

Panel 1:
- Good morning, Mother...!!
- Good morning, Son! Did you **brush** your **teeth**? Did you take a **bath**? Are you wearing **clean underwear** in case you have a **space accident**?
- I think we made a **bad mistake**—nicknaming the computer "**Mother!**" The darn machine is **carrying the role too far!!**

(Sign: MOTHER, THE DISCO COMPUTER BY LITE LAB)

Panel 2:
- Calling **Antarctica Control**... Calling **Antarctica Control**... This is Space Tug "**Noisy Roamer**"... Do you **read??** **Come in,** Antarctica!
- **Save** your **breath!** We're **nowhere near** home! When certain conditions arise, Mother **changes our course!** Those conditions have **arisen!**
- I bet we're supposed to **stay** out here in **space** until the **price** of the **oil ore** we're carrying **doubles!** The oil companies make us **do** that every few years or so!

ARTIST: MORT DRUCKER   WRITER: DICK DE BARTOLO

Panel 3:
- Mother has intercepted transmissions of **unknown origin!** She's already diverted our space tug to **investigate!** We'll probably be settling down into a **hostile environment** where they'll be speaking a **mysterious language!**
- Oh, boy... We're going to Washington, D.C....!

Panel 4:
- Ready for "**Undocking**"...!
- Set all gauges to **450°**...! Turn microwave to "**latch!**" Activate **teflon pans**...! Grease **cookie sheets,** and—
- I hate to **interrupt** during the **countdown,** Dripley... but I believe you're reading the ship's "**Cookbook**" not the ship's "**Manual!**"!
- **Too late!** Hang on!! I already pushed "**GRATE & CHOP!**"

117

KATCHOOM!

Y'know, that wasn't a bad landing... considering I made one little mistake!

Using the Cook Book?!?

No, using the WRONG PART of the ship!

We all should be in the OTHER part! The LANDER!!

Asp... what can you tell me about the atmosphere of this planet?

It contains oxygen!

Then, why must we wear our special breathing apparatus?

Because we people from Earth have adjusted ourselves to breathing in carbon monoxide, sulphur, asbestos dust and radioactive particles to stay alive!

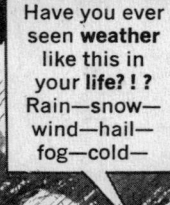

Have you ever seen weather like this in your life?!? Rain—snow—wind—hail—fog—cold—

It must be Sunday here! The weather is always like this on Sunday! And I bet if this place is inhabited, they were planning a picnic!

It's a skeleton of some alien creature! And look at its stomach! It appears to have exploded outward...!!

Well, we know one thing for certain! Where we are, they sure sell pepperoni pizza! Because only a pepperoni pizza could do stomach damage like THAT!

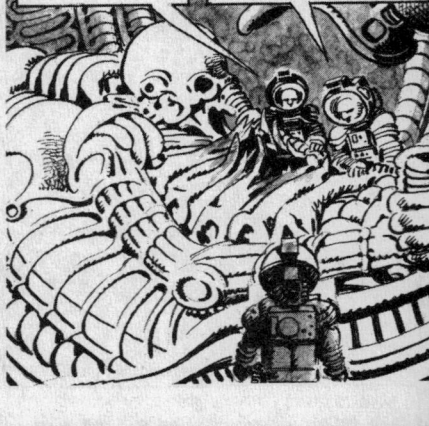

I found something! It's a cargo hold of some sort...!

Are you sure?!?

Positive! I just fell in!!

There's something strange down here... some kind of eggs! They're pale green and covered with a light blue mist...

This is no alien space ship!! This is where the Easter Bunny lives!

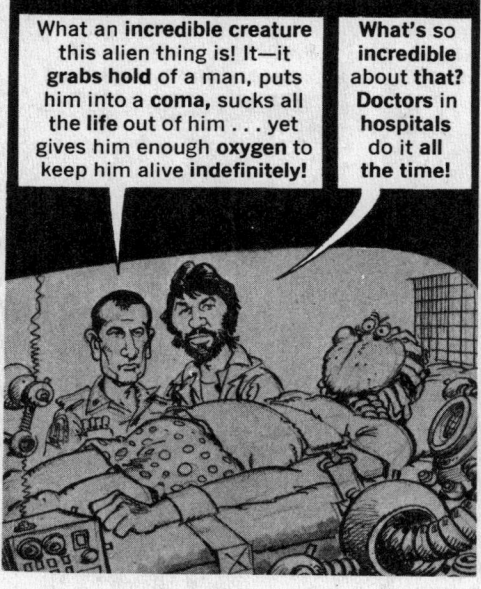

Panel 1: Asp, Mother has deciphered part of that mysterious message! It's **NOT** an S.O.S.!! It's a **warning** of some sort! I'd better go out and **warn** them before it's **too late**!

By the time you suit up and find them, they'll **KNOW** if something is wrong!!

You're right!! I'll warn them **AFTER** it's too late!

Panel 2: Dripley, open the **hatch**! Something has happened to **Pain** ...!! What **is** it?

We **don't know!** He just keeps **mumbling**! I **can't let you in** until you're **more specific**! Exactly **what happened** ...?

We **don't know** for sure! We **DO know**, whatever it is, it was terribly embarrassing for Pain! He keeps saying something about having **EGG** all over his face!!

Panel 3: **That idiot!!** When he said he'd found something in the cargo hold, I told him to **examine it closely** ... but **this** is **ridiculous!** And whatever it is, it **won't come off!** What are we gonna **do**?

Beats me! We could **paint it BLACK** and tell people he grew a **BEARD!**

Panel 4: What an **incredible creature** this alien thing is! It—it **grabs hold** of a man, puts him into a **coma**, sucks all the **life** out of him ... yet gives him enough **oxygen** to keep him alive **indefinitely!**

What's so incredible about **that**? **Doctors** in **hospitals** do it all the time!

Panel 5: My God! **Look!** I cut one of the thing's **legs** off, and the **stuff** that came out **ate** right through the floor!!

Are you **sure** the stuff came from the **creature?!** I spilled a can of **Diet Cola** here a while back, and you **KNOW** what **THAT** can do!!

Panel 6: It's amazing! The thing has **ACID** for **BLOOD**!!

That's **great!** Maybe we can kill him with a **ROLAID**!!

Panel 7: How's our creepy guest!?

I'm fine, Dripley!

I meant the **OTHER** creepy guest ... that **THING**!!

It disappeared! The only thing I'm **certain** of is, it's **NOT** in the Medical Supply Cabinet!

In that case, **I'LL** search for him in the Medical Supply Cabinet! The **REST** of you, search the **other** parts of the ship! And **good luck!**

119

THERE he is!
GET HIM! !
GET HIM! !
That's the CAT . . . you idiot!
Well, why in the world did we ever bring a CAT into space with us?
For companionship . . . and to create sudden scary effects!
EEOOW!
Here it is! I found it! It's DEAD! !
Good! Let's get that yecchy thing OUT of here!
Are you crazy? ! This thing is one of a kind! ! A rare species! I'm taking it back to Earth! !
Whatever FOR? ! ?
To put in people's drawers, and down women's dresses! ! This yecchy thing will scare people silly! It has the WHOOPEE CUSHION beat by a MILE! !
It—it MOVED!!
That's only a reflex action. You know what a reflex action is, don't you?
Yeah . . . what Dripley is doing right now . . . BARFING!
Dullest . . . why are you letting Asp keep that disgusting thing on this ship?
Because he has a title on this ship, and it's that title which authorizes him to take such action!
And what title is that . . . ?
Chief Officer In Charge Of Making Stupid Decisions!
Okay, it's time to blast off this God-forsaken planet! Ready, everybody?
Altering radar vectors . . . Retracting landing struts . . . energizing rockets . . .
Dripley, why are you going through all those complicated procedures, when all you have to do it just push the switch marked "Auto Blast Off?"
Because we NEED all the dialogue we can GET! This is a two-hour movie, and it's got six minutes of dialogue! !
You made a miraculous recovery, Pain! How do you feel . . . ?
Fine! Just fine! But, boy . . . am I HUNGRY! ! I'm so hungry, I—I could eat a MONSTER!
Slurp . . . crunch . . .
I think he's forgotten his manners! He's eating with his HANDS!
That's only because he ALREADY ATE his silverware!
I—I . . . Belch . . .
Gaggh . . . Choke . . . BARF . . .
SCREEAM!
It he's playing "Charades," my guess is he's acting out "The Exorcist!"
ACTING it out, I don't mind! HEAVING it out is a bit nauseating!
God, he's giving BIRTH!
Pain, I'm putting you on report! ! I TOLD everyone on this ship I wanted them on Birth Control Pills! !

What WAS that ugly hideous thing? !
All I know is . . . it wasn't MINE! ! It didn't have my eyes, or my nose, or my beard . . . or ANYTHING! !
I . . . I can't stop sobbing!
Don't be jealous, Lambaste!
Someday, you'll have a baby of your OWN! !
Whatever it is . . . it killed Pain! And now it's loose in the ship . . . and I'm SCARED!
Oh, don't be such a baby! Now, get some sleep, and we'll look for it in the morning! Good night, everybody!
Good night, Dull!
Good night, Bark!
Good night, Drip!
Good night, Frett!
And don't anybody get up to go to the bathroom without the other five!
I've heard of "Burials at Sea" . . . but this is my first "Burial at Space" . . .
I know that the FIRST thing that flew out was PAIN . . . but what was the OTHER thing?
His tombstone! The Captain wanted it to be a "proper burial!"!
RIP
ONE WAY
'BYE
THIS WAY
Okay, here's a weapon for each of you! It's a portable Cattle Prod! It's insulated here . . .
. . . and here . . .
. . . and here . . .
BUT NOT HERE!!
And this is a special "Tracking Device"! If you get within ten feet of the monster, micro-changes in air density sets it off!
I don't need that! I've got my OWN Scientific Device! If I get within ten feet of the monster, I pee in my pants!
I don't mind when Jokes—the cat—eats left-overs . . . but THIS is ridiculous!
Wait a minute! I think I see the cat in the ventilating system! Or IS it the cat?!
Let me try and remember! Was our cat eight feet tall . . . and hideously ugly?
GORE!
Frett is dead!
Did the thing get him . . .??
Well, sort of! He WET himself to death!

Panel 1:
- We KNOW he's in the ventilating system!! Now, what do we do?
- I say cut off his air!
- I say cut off his heat!
- I say raise his rent!
- We're trying to kill a monster—not evict a tenant!

Panel 2:
- I have a reading on you, Dullest! I know exactly where, in the ventilating system, you are!
- Are you sure?!?
- I'm positive! By the way, WHICH dot are you?!?
- Whaddya mean . . . "Which dot?" I'm here alone! I'm the ONLY dot!!
- Well, I see TWO DOTS, so—unless you have a split personality, I suggest you start running and screaming!
- BLOOD!

Panel 3:
- First . . . the thing got Pain—and now Frett and Dullest are gone!
- Yeah! And you want to know something? Considering that ". . . in space, no one can hear you scream," they made a hell of a racket!

Panel 4:
- What's REALLY going on here, Mother? Tell me the TRUTH!
- All alien life must be brought back to Earth, even if the entire crew has to be sacrificed!
- Boy . . . now I know why they call you "Mother" . . . you MOTHER!!

Panel 5:
- Now, now! Let's not be upset with Mother!
- You knew, you creep! You knew we were to be sacrificed! You—you're nothing but a company man, working hand in hand with that lousy computer!
- Well, not exactly hand in hand . . . ! More like transistor in transistor!
- SOK!

Panel 6:
- Will you look at that! Asp is a robot!
- No wonder he never reacted to me as a woman!
- I got news for you!! I'm NOT a robot, and you never really turned ME on, either!

Panel 7:
- I always suspected Asp was a robot! He was the only one of us who called the computer "Mother" like he meant it!
- Reconnect his vocal chords so I can ask him how we kill the thing!
- You CAN'T!! It has a structural perfection never matched by any other human being!
- Evidentally, Asp, you've never seen Dolly Parton!
- Okay, Asp, if you won't help us, I'm pulling your plug!
- Big deal! I already PULLED YOURS!!

I'm putting the ship on "Auto Detonation" to blow it up! We'll escape in the Lander! You two, go below and get all the fuel and food you can carry!
I'll go look for Jokes, the cat!
That cat has scared the life out of me six times already!
Well, he STILL has three lives to go!
Let's not pile TOO many things on this cart! I want to be able to go through "Express Check-Out"!
Let's see! So far, we've got fuel, vitamins, coffee, monster, eggs, milk—ulp! MONSTER?!
Good Lord!! When I said "Express CHECK-OUT," I didn't mean my L—I—F—E!
BLECCH
Well, the monster got Barker and Lambaste . . . and I'm all alone on this Lander! So . . . since there's no one left to talk to, I guess I'll strip off all my clothes to keep the audience entertained . . .
Boy, I just got a look at myself in the mirror, and I look terrible! My hair is a mess . . . my make-up is smeared . . . my tentacles are wrinkled . . . my stainless teeth need brushing—
Oh, NO!! It's followed me into the Lander! It seems determined to kill every last one of us! It must be a MOVIE CRITIC!
I know! I'll give it the old "Look out the window at the fantastic view from up here!" routine, and then I'll blast him off into outer space!!
This is Dripley, reporting . . . I've blasted the monster into space, and now I'm going to get into my sleep pod for the six month trip back to Earth!
We've got NEWS for you, Dripley, You're only SIX MINUTES from Earth!
Look! Up in the sky!
It's a bird!
It's a plane!
It's Superman!
Superman doesn't have a stainless steel cape . . . !!
It's SUPER ALIEN!!
Somebody's gonna pay for this!
Yeah! US!

EVERYBODY'S GAWKIN' DEPT.

The following article is rated "G"...which means it's Okay for General Audiences. However, the following article is a MAD satire of an "X"-rated movie...which means the movie is dirty, and Children Under 16 are Not Permitted to see it. Which further means that if you are under 16, you couldn't possibly have seen the movie, and therefore you cannot possibly enjoy this MAD satire

MIDNIGHT

ARTIST: MORT DRUCKER

Well, Sam... I'm leavin' Texas, an' I'm a-headin' for New York... where I can do plenny of huggin' an' kissin'!

Why you wanna go to New York, Joe? You do plenny of huggin' an' kissin' right here!

Yeah, but I'm **tired** of huggin' an' kissin' **COWS**! I'm talkin' about huggin' an' kissin' **WOMEN** for a change!

Be careful, Joe! New York is a **rough place** for an out-of-towner!

How they gonna **know** I'm from out of town? I saved up all year an' bought me this City Slicker outfit!

Besides, with my Award-Winning Lips, I'll drive them New York women **crazy**! So long, Sam . . .

So, long, Joe Cluck! An' remember . . . dress your lips **warm**!

124

of it. So use your dopey, under-16 head for a change! Don't laugh at this article if your parents are around, or you'll give it away that you lied about your age and sneaked in to see the movie! (Incidentally, if your parents laugh at this article, it means they must have seen the movie, and you can ask them what in heck they were doing, going to see a dirty movie anyhow!) Here, then, is...

WOWBOY

WRITER: STAN HART

Hey, driver! How long will it take to get to New York City?

It's 36 hours to the big city, son!

Gee, what'll I do t' pass the time?

Why don't you amuse yourself by thinking up some interesting flash-backs?

I never did this before, Joe! I'm not that kind of a girl!

Well, just relax an' enjoy it, Baby—because you're being loved by the GREATEST!

THE GREATEST?? Gee, I don't know about that! Let's just say you're in the TOP TEN!!

I'll never amount t nuthin' aroun' here, Gran'ma!

Don't be so impatient with yourself, Joey! You already got seven girls into trouble! That's only three shy of the County record for August!

Yeah, but I want t' be the BEST!

Well, you still got two whole days left! Work at it!

Gee! New York shor is an unfriendly town! Isn't New York an unfriendly town?

I wouldn't know, Dummy! This is Chicago!

Hey, driver! How many more hours to New York City?
Twenty-four!
Gosh! I'm all out of flash-backs! Could I use one of yours?
Golly, gee, New York is such a heartless city! I wonder why nobody wants to help this man?!
Hey, mister! Are you okay? What's your name?
John Lindsay—and you must be from out of town!
Hey, Honey! How about we go up to your place for some wild huggin' an' kissin'?
Get lost!
Hmmm! Next time, I think I'll try the direct approach!
Er—uh—could I ask you a question, Ma'am?
Sure, Texas! Fire away!
Do you always do this with the television set on?
Yep! That way, if you're not a great lover, I'm not bored!
Well? What do you think?
Will you turn up the sound?
HELLO! HELLO!
Let's see—that's ten assorted hugs at $1.00 each . . . an' seven juicy kisses at $1.50 each . . . an' two hickies at $3.00 each! Which means you owe me $26.50!
What?! You expect me to pay that??
Yes, Ma'am! Y'know . . . chapsticks don't grow on trees!
What happened?
You must've done somethin'!
I dunno! She threw me out!
All I did was charge her $3.00 each for two hickies!
$3.00!?? Dummy!! She's a New Yorker! She gets hickies WHOLESALE!!

Hey, Rube! What are you supposed to be?
What do I look like? I'm a great lover! I drive women crazy! I'm gonna make a fortune!
HOTEL ROOMS
RITZ
BAR
Y'know what, Joe Cluck? You need a promoter! An' I, Ratface Ratfink, just happen to be the greatest promoter in New York City!
No kiddin'?
Listen, y'know the Brooklyn Bridge . . . ?
Well, this morning, I closed a deal on it!
You sold the Brooklyn Bridge?!?
No, I BOUGHT it!
Wow!!
GOING OUT OF BUSINESS SALE!
BOWLI
WALK
ATTENTION ALL LADIES
Need Loving?
TRY
Joe Cluck
KISSING & HUGGING
2 LIPS 2
No Waiting!
NOW PLAYING
I can make you famous, Joe! You'll be the toast of the nation . . .
I wanna thank the Academy for this honor! An' I wanna thank my two lips, without whose help, this would never have been possible!
You'll be immortalized in cement outside Grauman's Theater . . .
Gee! My lip-prints . . . right next to Trigger's hoof-prints!
You could even be President! There'd be no stopping you . . .
JOE CLUCK for PRESIDE
ELECT CLUCK FOR PRESIDENT
Me, Joey! Kiss ME!! Don't waste those marvelous lips on KIDS! What do they know!?
I'm gonna introduce you to a guy who's looking for a talent like you! Just gi'me $20.00 for my trouble!
Gee! $20.00 is a lot of money!
If you're gonna think small, Joe, you're gonna stay small!
Why, only yesterday I shelled out TWICE that much for a downpayment on The Statue of Liberty!
FLOWER SHO

So you want to save lonely, unhappy women from leading fruitless, desperate, barren lives?
Yep! I shor do!
Well, I've got just the assignment for you . . .
B-But . . . I don't think you quite understand!
Shut up and hit that Bass Drum! I thought you wanted to do God's work!
Well, not exactly! What I really had in mind was goin' into business for myself!
Look, Selma! They're filming another movie with authentic backgrounds right here on the streets of New York City!
Just stare right into the camera naturally!
Hey, mister—I'll give you a dollar if you'll go into this movie and sit with me and hold my hand! I'm—I'm scared of Horror Pictures!
Me, too, kid . . . but, okay! I need the money!
NOW PLAYING
Gee, I hate all the hitting and stomping and punching and violence and bloodshed you see in movie theaters these days!
But there wasn't any of that stuff in the picture we just saw!
I'm not talking about in the picture! I'm talking about in HERE . . . when you find out I don't have the dollar I promised you!
I know it's a crummy-lookin' joint, Joe—Cough! Cough!—but I'm only stayin' here till I can get to Miami—Cough! Cough!
Hey, ain't you worried about that cough, Ratface?
Yeah, dammit! It's getting BETTER! An' just when I'm up for a part in an "Anti-Smoking Commercial"!
Hey, handsome! How would you like to go to a party?
What kinda party?
A "pot" party!
Naw! those Tupperware affairs are a big bore!
Boy! He's some dummy!

Gee, Ratface, I never **saw** a party like **this** before!
It's a cinch you don't go to the **movies** very often! There's a **psychedelic drug scene** in **EVERY "NOW" FILM** these days!
Hey, Joe! **You okay?** What's the **matter?**
I'm havin'a **bad trip,** Ratface! I keep imaginin' I'm an **Accountant** in **Teaneck, New Jersey!**
That's the deal! **Take it** or **leave it!** My boy, here, will give you **your choice** of **one from Column A** and **two from Column B** for **$18.75.** And we'll throw in **one Fox Trot with an occasional dip** for **FREE!**
Okay, it's a deal! I'll **take** it! Let's go!
Don't feel bad, Joe! It **happens,** sometimes!
It's never happened to **me** before! I'm **washed up—finished!** I **can't pucker!** My—my **lips** are **gone!**
Think of **pickles!**
Think of **lemons!**
Think of **pickled lemons!**
See, Joe? You **did** it! **You did it!**
You're **wonderful . . .** jus' **wonderful!** You're so wonderful, I'm gonna give you a **twenty percent discount!**

I mean it, Gladys! He's fantastic! But you'd better hurry up and make up your mind! I've almost got him booked solid! Wednesday, he kisses the Ladies Bridge Club! Thursday, he gives hickies to the PTA! And Friday, he catering a Wedding! He's scheduled to blow in the ear of the entire Groom's side!
Gee, I can't stop thinkin' of them pickled lemons!
I'm sick, Joe! I gotta get to Miami! I'll die if I don't!
I'll get the money, Ratface—somehow!
Listen, Joey! Will you do me a favor? When we're in Miami Beach, will you call me by my right name . . . Ruggerio Ruccici!?
I'll do you a bigger favor, Ratface! When we're in Miami Beach, I'll call you by an even better name . . . Irving Weinstein!!
Son, I'll give you $20 if you'll just sit there and stay awake while I talk to you!
$20?! Just to listen?!
That's right! Y'see, I'm an Economics Teacher, and I want someone, just once, to stay awake while I'm lecturing!
Now, the Mathusian Theory . . .
If we consider Gresham's Law . . .
The fallacy of Keynsian Economics is simply . . .
YOU SADIST . . . EXPECTING ANYONE TO STAY AWAKE DURING THAT!!
Stop! Wait! You haven't heard about the Federal Reserve System!!
I gotta get to Miami, Joe!
Just hang on, Ratface! We'll be there soon! Here's the bus!
It's YOU again! Hey, I thought of some great flash-backs for you!
BROOKLY
N325
69
BUS
BD 673
Are we almost there, Joe? Are we almost in Miami?
Yes! We're almost . . . OH-OH!!
What's the matter?
I don't think we're gonna make it to Miami, Ratface!
Why not, Joe??
The bus is being hijacked to Cuba!!
250

No. 169

MAD

I.Q.
130
120
110
100
90
80
70
60
50

SPECIAL COP OUT ISSUE
SERPICOOL AND McCLOD

WAYNE ON THE WANE DEPT.

There's a new "John Wayne" movie around in which John Wayne *dies!* Sure, he died in lots of other movies, but in this one, he dies of *bullets* ALONG WITH the *dialogue!* See what we mean in MAD's version of

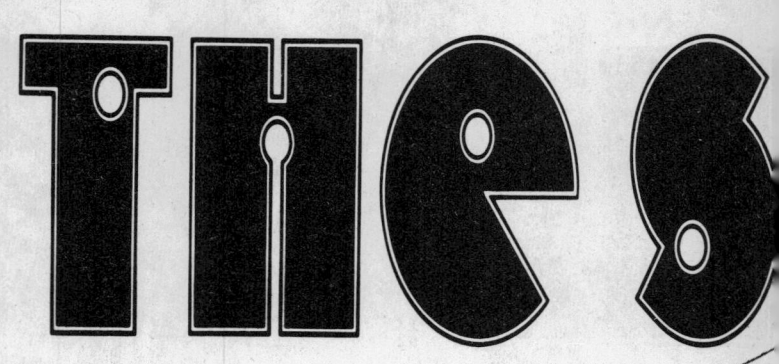

The S

Hey... move out of the way, you tired old son of a @#$%¢!!

C'mon, Slob... knock it off!! My Mom taught me to have a little respect for tired old sons of @#$%¢'s!

Hey, Mister! Wanna paper? Queen Victoria is dead!

Oh-oh! That's bad news! With my reputation, they'll probably blame it on me!

Well, if it isn't one of my worst enemies.... J. B. Dukes! I should shoot him dead right here, but he DOES look tired! I'll just let him take a nap... and then maybe I can shoot him in his sleep!

Look who just rode in! J. B. Dukes, the famous shootist! I been after his hide for years, an' now my big chance is getting closer! Yep, my timing is better... an' his arthritis is worse!

Looks like trouble just rode into town, Sheriff!

I'm not worried! There's an empty cell in the jail! I'll just lock myself inside it!

HOOTIEST

ARTIST: MORT DRUCKER WRITER: DICK DE BARTOLO

Okay, Doctor Horsefeathers, you've gone over me with a fine-toothed comb! Now, give it to me straight... How bad is it?

Well, le'me put it this way! If you don't pay me my fee by Friday, I'm out $5.00!

Will I be able to carry on my normal life till then?

Sure you can! Shoot-outs... Hangings... Fist-fights... They're all fine! Just try not to EXERT yourself!!

Just one more thing, Doc! I took this pillow from a Bordello! Is it okay if I continue... you know!... Is it okay if... when I feel like it... well... Awww... you know what I mean, Doc...

Sure! Sure! Keep stealin' pillows as long as you like!!

Howdy, Ma'am! Ol' Doc Horsefeathers said you might have a room for me to rent...!

How long do you plan on staying?

For the rest of my life!

Sorry! I only have a room available for ONE WEEK!

That should do it!!

This is a modern house with all of the modern conveniences! Here is the telephone... and here is the bathroom with a tub and complete indoor plumbing...

That's great! First, I'd like to make a phone call, and then I'd like to take a bath!

Well, the phone is out of order, and there's no more hot water!

Boy, this house really is modern!

133

As long as you're staying, I'd like to know your name!
Er . . . my name is Wong Ling Chow!
And your business?
I'm a Chinese Laundryman!
Well, you sound very honest!
Just chalk it up to my Oriental inscrutability!
Do you have room to bed down and feed one more?
Sure! Take any stall! And how about a place for your horse?!
Hey! That horse belongs to J.B. Dukes, the West's most famous SHOOTIST!!
How do you know for sure?
You silly fool! Everybody knows his horse is brown!
Mom! Do you know who's staying in this very house?!?
Of course! Wong Ling Chow, the Chinese Laundry-man!
Wong Ling Chow . . .?!? It's J. B. DUKES, the famous GUN-SHOOTIST!! Gee, he owes you an apology for lying!
He ALSO owes me a sheet and two pillow cases that I gave him to launder!
Mr. Dukes, I want you out of my house!
Oh, come on! I know last night's dinner wasn't GREAT . . . but that's ridiculous!
I can't go! I'm going to DIE here!
You don't understand! I have a CANCER . . .!
In that case . . . there's only one Christian thing to do! I'll have to change your rent from "WEEKLY" to "HOURLY"!
I knew you were in town, Dukes . . . and I was gonna run you out! Then, I heard about your sickness! So I brought you something to cure it!
Sheriff, nothing can cure a Cancer!
This can . . . but you'll really have to shake it well before you use it! It's a RATTLESNAKE!
I'm Bobkins from "The Daily Press"!
If you're here to sell subscriptions, you better have a special 3-day rate!
No, Mr. Dukes! I'm here to do your life story! I can guarantee it'll hit the FRONT PAGE!
Oh, yeah? How can you guarantee that . . .?!?
Because "The Daily Press" is a very small paper! We only HAVE a front page!!

Panel 1:
- Mr. Dukes, I want to do a **totally factual** account of your life! No lies, no dressings, just the plain, honest, unvarnished truth!
- So... I'll make it up!
- I don't have the time to tell it all to you!
- Okay! But now you're **never** going to see your name in our newspaper!
- Do you have an Obituary column?
- Yes...
- Get out!!
- Wanna BET?!?

(Sign: RANDY SELTZER AND FATHER INC.)

Panel 2:
- Doc... I want you to tell me straight out! How **bad** is it gonna get?
- Well, it's gonna hit your **spine** and **hips** first! Then... your **groin**! You won't be able to **stand** after a while! Your **head** will start to **throb**, and your **ears** will feel like they're **exploding off your skull**! You'll be **screaming out loud** a lot in **sheer agony**! And then the PAIN will start!
- Then the pain will START?!? What's all that other stuff?!?
- Severe symptoms!

Panel 3:
- Bland, come with me for a ride in the country!
- No! I—I couldn't! I've only been a Widow for a year!
- We could look at the trees, and the lakes, and the birds, and flowers—
- No! I—I can't!
- And we could fool around a little in the bushes...!
- I'll be ready to leave promptly at 8:00, J. B....!

Panel 4:
- Some day, I hope to have a little plot of land like that...
- I'm glad to see you're not thinking about death! That IS a lovely farm down there!
- I'm talking about the place across the road! That CEMETERY!!
- Now, now, J. B.! By the way... exactly what does J. B. stand for?
- Jane Belle!
- No wonder you're so good at defending yourself!

Panel 5:
- Mr. Dukes! What is going on in here?!?
- One guy came through **that** window with a knife, and one guy came through **that** window with a shotgun! They tried to kill Mr. Dukes, but **he** got them first!
- Mr. Dukes... when you moved in, I specifically told you, "No entertaining in the rooms!"

Panel 6:
- Well, your reputation has finally forced my two other tenants to move out! They were afraid that living in the same house with you would give them each a bad name!
- C'mon! My reputation can't be THAT bad!!
- Wanna bet? One of my tenants was a CARD SHARK and the other was a PROSTITUTE!

Panel 1
Killem... how dare you try to sell my horse without my consent?!?
I was only trying to help my Mom! You're five hours behind in the rent, y'know...!
In that case, I forgive you! How would you like me to give you a shooting lesson?
Great! But you'll have to use MY GUNS! I sold yours!

Panel 2
Wow! Six bullet holes... in a perfect, straight line!!
That's why they call me "The World's Greatest Shootist"!!
Then I wonder what they're gonna call ME?!? Those are MY SIX SHOTS!! Yours all MISSED!!

Panel 3
What do you **mean**, you want to charge $50 to bury me?!? You'll make **ten times** that amount from the people who'll want to see me dead! No... you'll pay ME $100!
Okay! Okay! Boy, thirty years in the Undertaking business, and this is the first time I've ever had an argument on price with the CORPSE!!

Panel 4
Gee, Mr. Dukes, thanks a lot for giving me permission to sell these locks of hair that I just trimmed off your head as SOUVENIRS!
You go right ahead! I don't mind! It's just that—well—are you sure all that hair is from ME?!?

GET A REAL LOCK OF J.B. DUKES' HAIR — YOUR CHOICE OF COLORS AND LENGTHS

Panel 5
Killem, I want you to run an errand for me! I want you to go find the **three men I hate the most**, and tell them to be at The Silver Nugget Saloon on Monday morning at 11:00!
Boy, you're some brave man!
Not really! Because on Monday morning at 11:00, I'LL be at the Golden Slipper Saloon!

Panel 6
Mr. Dukes, here's the tombstone you ordered! I'm real sorry, but they forgot to put the DATE on it!
And they ALSO forgot to put your NAME on it!
And they ALSO forgot to SHAPE it like a tombstone!
In other words... you just brought me a big, flat ROCK!!

Hi, Mom! I—Hey! What are you two doing in there?!?
Now, don't get the wrong idea, Killem! I'm just helping J. B. out of the tub!
Oh, great! I was WONDERING when you two were gonna get into something kinky!
I'll have you know Mr. Dukes is in the tub FULLY DRESSED!
Wow!! That IS kinky!!
Today's my birthday, Bartender . . . so give me a shot of the best whiskey in the house!!
BLAM
VIP!
Oh, nuts! Don't tell me I accidentally walked into the SILVER NUGGET SALOON . . . !?!
Hey, Old Man! Take that . . . and that . . . and that . . .
BLAM
Did you see that?! The bullets just bounced off J. B. Dukes! That's nerves of steel!!
Nerves of steel, NOTHING! That's HARDENING OF THE ARTERIES!!
BAM
BLAM
BLAM! BLAM! BLAM!
SALOON
You . . . you killed all three of them, J. B.!! But I—I don't understand! I thought you wanted them to kill YOU . . . to put you out of your misery!!
That's right! That's what I wanted! But then, that ol' BUG-A-BOO took over!
What was that . . . ?
FORCE OF HABIT!
Lucky for me, the Bartender snuck up and shot me in the back!!
If you came to patch up Mr. Dukes, you're too late, Doc!
I didn't come to patch him up! I came to give him good news! The lab report arrived from Dodge City! He doesn't have a Cancer after all! It was one of those tiny little mistakes in diagnosis! What he's got is an acute case of constipation!
But, Doc . . . he's DEAD!!
Well, y'know how these acute cases of constipation can get out of hand! Tell him to take two aspirins, and call me in the morning . . . !!

PLAYING IT FOR SHARK VALUE DEPT.

There's a sick new trend in movies! It started with "Airport", continued with "Towering Inferno", sunk to a low with "Earthquake" and has now reached the depths with the movie that's REALLY packing 'em in, the one about a giant shark that terrorizes a summer community! Yep, it's obvious that people get their kicks out of seeing other people die... in every horrible way possible, which includes being...

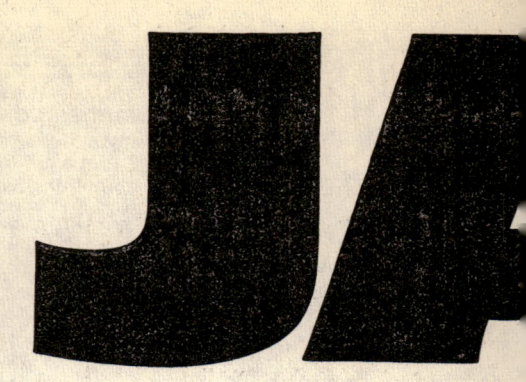

JA

Well, here we are... a bunch of **teenagers** *enjoying a* **typical Summer night** *in the typical seaside community of* **Vomity, Long Island!**

It sure is **fun** *sitting on a cool beach, drinking beer... smoking pot... listening to Rock... and making out!*

Yeah, but the first thing you know... it'll be **September** *and we'll be back in* **school,** *and our* **whole lives'll change!**

Yeah! What **a drag...** *sittin' in a hot* **classroom,** *drinking beer... smoking pot... listening to Rock... and making out!*

Maybe **you're** *having fun... but* **I'm bored!** *Doesn't anything* **different** *ever happen on this beach?*

Like **I said,** *... doesn't anything* **DIFFERENT** *happen on this beach?!*

Look at Freddy and Brenda... running to go swimming nude and then make out in the water!

What's that **strange THING** *out there?!*

Yeah... and listen to that rich, melodic background music...!

Oh, my God, it's horrible! HORRIBLE!

That **strange thing** *out there...?*

*No—***melodic music!** *I never* **heard** *music with a* **melody** *before!* **Quick!** *Someone turn up that* **Rock number** *before I go* **crazy!**

AW'D

ARTIST: MORT DRUCKER WRITER: LARRY SIEGEL

My ankle! He's got me by the ankle!

Man, that Freddie is really somethin' else!

Wow! Ankle-biting! What a wild, crazy turn-on!

Frankly, I'm worried about Brenda... all the way out there with Freddie... YOU'RE worried! I'm FREDDIE!!

What do we know about this reported missing person....?

The description I got, Chief, was that it's a teenager... shoulder-length hair, wearing earrings...

Is it a boy or a girl?

Aw— c'mon now, Chief!

Look! Nowadays that description is no proof one way or the other!

We KNOW it's a girl, Chief! When she was last seen, she was NAKED!

I got NEWS for you! Nowadays, THAT's no proof either!

What do you think could have happened to her, Chief?

I hate to say it, but if you've been around here as long as I have, you've seen those hideous, ugly monsters... attacking everything in sight...

I know! I've been in the halls of the High School!

And then again, if we're lucky, maybe it was only a SHARK!

I... choke... I found something... Chief!!

Is it—what—you thought it was??

Ugh... ecch... it's what I thought it was... all right!!

Listen to me! Get hold of yourself! You're a Police Officer! You can stand up to anything, even the remains of a body after a shark gets through with it!

Oh, yeah? How about the typical garbage left behind by the slobs after an all night beach party?!

Oh, God! Anything but that!

139

Uggh! Melon rinds and banana peels!
Blaah! Anchovy pizza scraps and scungili!
Pyuch! Peanut butter sandwiches and —
What do you think you're doing, Chief Brooding?!?
The remains of a girl were found, Mayor Vault! She must have been eaten by a shark! We can't allow any people in the water!
Are you insane?! Close our beaches with July 4th a week away?! That's when we do all our business around here! Forget about that shark and take down that sign!
Forget about it?! Do you realize what horror you may be subjecting people to on this beach? Have you no conscience? Particularly on Independence Day, when Americans celebrate their precious, hard-earned freedom by blowing off their arms and legs with firecrackers, and driving drunkenly down our nation's highways . . .
Come to think of it, I guess I'll take down the sign!
NO SWIMMING ON THIS BEACH
By Order of Vomity P.D.
INCORPORATED TOWNSHIP OF VO
POPULATION..... 3,013 2
How come we're all enjoying ourselves, and the Chief of Police has to work?
They say a mysterious thing is endangering the beach, and he's protecting all of us!
It must be tough looking through those glasses hours on end!
What dedication! I'm sure that whatever he's looking for, he's going to GET it!
Not unless somebody tells his WIFE!!
Well, Schmendricks, so far . . . so good!
That's great! No sign of the shark?
No sign of her Husband!
What happened?
All of a sudden I heard this rich melodic music, and then this kid started screaming and . . . ugh . . . it was just awful . . . !
Yecch! All that blood and gore and torn limbs! You know what this means, don't you, Chief . . .?
Right! There goes the picture's "G" rating! But a "PG" will still pull in the kids . . .!
What about that line in the ads that says, "May Be Too Intense For Younger Children"? Won't that hurt us?
Are you kidding?!? That's like trying to scare ants away from a picnic by pouring sugar on the ground!
I've called this meeting of you key townspeople because there is a silly rumor going around that an alleged shark has allegedly killed two alleged people! We will now have the Coroner's report! Er . . . where is the Coroner?
He's dead!
WHAT?! How did it happen?
The alleged shark bit off his alleged head! Also his alleged arms and legs . . .

Panel 1:
Very well! The meeting is open to suggestions! Would anyone like to speak...?

AAARRRGH!
SHRIEK!
YEOW!

SCREEEECHHH

Does Captain Squint always do disgusting things like that for attention?

No... he usually just belches!

Panel 2:
Now, listen to me, Matey... and listen good! I'm the only Sea Captain around here who can CATCH that mother, and you know it! But it's gonna cost you ten thousand dollars!

Take it... or leave it! And the more you wait, the more it's gonna cost you! And if you don't like my offer, you and this whole #★⊘❀&.✦★!! town can go #★⊘❀&.✦★!!

Panel 3:
We'll think about it, Captain Squint!

Does he actually make a living as a Sea Captain?

Not really! He moonlights on the side!

What's his other job?

He works for The Welcome Wagon!

Panel 4:
We're in trouble, Schmendricks! The Mayor is still not sold on the shark story, and I'm not sure I trust Squint! Isn't there ANYONE who can help us?!?

Hi, there! I'd like to help! My name is Clod Hopper, and I'm a brilliant young Scientist! I know ALL ABOUT sharks! God, but they're beautiful creatures! Do you know that I once made LOVE to a shark?! I mean... this one really turned me on, and—

What?!? How could ANYONE make love to a shark!!

Very carefully!

Panel 5:
Hmmm! I notice—as I scientifically examine the remains of this victim—that the thorax and the upper anatomy in general, particularly the sternum and scapula, have been severely traumatized, and that the metatarsal bones on the severed foot that I hold in my hand have been nearly obliterated...

Uh-huh... Uh-huh... quite interesting! Now... after assimilating all this, there is one thing I'd like to say as a Scholar... and as a Scientist...

What's that...?

Panel 6:
YECCCH!

141

Great news, Chief! My kid and I caught the shark, so your troubles are over!
Incredible! How did you and your kid ever manage to land a fish this size?
Very simple! My kid has this old kite string, see? Well, sir . . . I bent this safety pin around the string and tossed it into the—
Wait a minute! You expect me to believe that anybody using a safety pin and some old kite string could catch a shark!?!
Sure, providing you use the right bait . . .!
And what did YOU use for bait?
My kid!
VOMITY YACHT CLUB
I'm not sure this is the shark we're after! The only way to know for sure is to cut him open and look for clues inside! Don't worry! I know what I'm doing! I've been around fish all my life . . .
You know, you remind me of a sturgeon!
You mean SURGEON! I cut like a surgeon!
You may CUT like a surgeon, but you SMELL like a sturgeon!
Ah-hah! Just as I thought! This shark doesn't eat people! It eats JUNK! Look at this! An old lawn mower, a pair of orthopedic shoes, a 1959 Edsel, a crate of watermelons and 500,000 copies of Reader's Digest!
Sew him up fast! I feel like we just operated on Euell Gibbons!
Mayor Vault! I've got proof that the dead shark is NOT the one we're after! The killer is STILL OUT THERE! We've got to close the beaches . . . NOW!!
Not on your life! This is July 4th! But don't worry! They're going to set up an impregnable barrier in the water that no shark will ever be able to penetrate!
It won't work! He's too smart! He'll slip past the gun boats! He'll sneak by the helicopters!
I KNOW that! I'm talking about the NATURAL barrier: that wall of typical holiday refuse and garbage . . . thrown into the water by 50,000 beachgoers!
ARRRRRGGHH!
YECCCCH!
CHOKE!
UGH!
Well . . . Mayor?!? Still MORE deaths! Are you satisfied now?!?
Okay, Chief! You win! I'll pay Squint what he wants! Go out there with him and GET THAT SHARK!!
Golly, all this blood and torn bodies and killer sharks! They sure don't make "Beach Pictures" the way I made them in the '60's!
That's true, Annette! But THIS one is ALMOST as nauseating as one of yours!
Now hear this, Mates! I'm the Captain of this@#$%¢& boat, and what I say GOES! I've been a sailor, man and boy, for forty years! I know every inch of this ocean and every nook and cranny of this boat! I know the sound and the smell and the language of the sea! And now, if you'll excuse me, I gotta go to The Little Boy's Room . . .
Don't you mean "The Head"?
Whatever.

Panel 1:
- I'd feel a lot more secure if he didn't get SEASICK!
- I'd feel even BETTER if we weren't still in PORT!!

Panel 2:
- The College Boy'll take the helm! And you, Chief... you see those pails of bloody fish innards and entrails? Well, start throwing it overboard...
- Oh, I get it! It's BAIT... to lure the shark!
- Naaahh! Sharks HATE the stuff!
- Then why do you want me to throw it overboard?
- You think I want it stinking up my boat?
- Then why'd you bring it aboard in the first place?
- Listen... one more stupid question, and I'll have you down on your hands and knees, swabbing the floor!!
- The "DECK"!
- Whatever.

Panel 3:
- Don't you sort of get the feeling we've been HAD?
- Not really! He may be a bit eccentric, but I think he's a good sailor! Let's wait until we're out a while and he gets his sea legs and starts singing those loveable old Sea Chanteys...
- ♪ Over hill, over dale, We have hit the Dusty trail, As those Caissons Go rolling along! ♪
- You're RIGHT! We've been HAD!

Panel 4:
- You see this scar? That's from a Tiger Shark when I was in the South Pacific!
- That's nothing! See THIS scar! That's from a Giant Barracuda when I was in Key Largo!
- That's nothing! See THIS scar! That's from Gene Hackman when I was in "The French Connection"!

Panel 5:
- C'mon, Squint... you're an expert on sharks! Tell us all about 'em!
- ♪ Oh, the shark has... Pretty teeth, dear... And he shows them... Pearly white... ♪
- Boy... with these Old Salts, everything is a SONG CUE!!

Panel 6:
- Well, we've been out for ten hours and still no sign of the shark! Where could he be? If there was only some way we knew he was in the area! If he would only give us some sort of clue!
- Wait a minute! Do you hear it? That rich, melodic music...??
- Yeah! Yeah! I hear it!!
- Does that mean anything to you?
- You bet...!

143

Hey . . . what the hell are you doing?!?
That's not dance music, dummy! It's the theme of the shark! It follows him wherever he goes!
For Pete's sake, will you please let me go, now!
I'm sorry! Okay . . . YOU lead!
He must be one of those rare Mantovani sharks!!
Give me one more minute! I'm a fantastic dipper!
What are YOU doing, Squint?
I see! And then, we FOLLOW him?
I'm shooting this harpoon . . . with a barrel tied to it . . . into him! That's so we'll know where he is at all times . . . and in what direction he's swimming!
No, then we go in the OTHER direction! A guy can get KILLED around here!!
Good Lord! Three harpoons in him . . . and he's still coming at us! I've got to admit . . . I'm STUMPED!!
You WILL be . . . if he sinks this boat!
Wait! I have an idea that just might save us—but it's not completely worked out yet! Why don't I climb into this cage, and you lower me into the water! That'll lure the shark toward me, and I'll kill him!
How will you KILL him?!?
Er—that's the part I haven't worked out yet!
Hey, I've got it! STRYCHNINE!! This poison will kill ANYTHING!
Great! Only HOW will you give it to the SHARK?!
Good question! Uh . . . I know! I know! Oh, it's so simple! Why didn't I think of this before! What I'll do is MIX TWO MARTINIS! Then, I'll propose a toast, and when the shark isn't looking, I'll slip some of this into HIS!
Why don't you just dip a NEEDLE into the poison . . . and shoot it at him?!
That's even better!
Here he comes . . .! This is it . . .! Oh, God . . . if only he holds still long enough . . .! If only he gives me a clear shot at his eye . . .!
If only I didn't drop the needle!!

Panel 1
He's back! He got **Clod!** The poison thing **didn't work!** What now, Captain?

You wait here while I go and check the old **Navy Manual** . . .

Panel 2
It's **too late** for that now! A desperate situation calls for **desperate measures!** *Er—* I **know!** Listen to **THIS** . . .

Panel 3
OKAY, SHARK . . . MY MEN HAVE YOU SURROUNDED! DROP YOUR TEETH AND COME OUT OF THE WATER WITH YOUR FINS UP AND YOU WON'T GET HURT . . .

Wait a minute, Shark! Not so **FAR** out of the water!!

Panel 4
Too bad! It always worked in **"COPS AND ROBBERS"** movies!

Panel 5
Well, Mate! I guess I'm a **goner!** But if I **gotta go,** I suppose it's only fit that an old sailor like me **die at sea!** So long, lad! This old sea dog is headed for his **final resting** place in **Davey Smith's Locker** . . .

That's Davey **JONES'S** Locker!

Panel 6
Whatever . . .

Well, there goes Squint! And **I'm next!!** Nothing can stop that shark now!

Panel 7
Hi! What's going **on?**

CLOD!! You're alive! **YOU'RE ALIVE . . . !!**

Panel 8
Uggh . . . Ooooh . . . . . . POOF . . .

And **LOOK!** The shark is **DEAD!**

Panel 9
It's a **miracle!** How did the shark **DIE?**

Psychological Indigestion!

What in hell is **that?**

It's a very rare **fish** disease, brought on by a very common **movie** disease that we **Scientists** call **"Scriptus Fantasticus!"**

C'mon, Man! Talk sense!

I think you **know** by now that a **shark** can usually **eat ANYTHING!** However, when he had me **underwater** . . . and he **destroyed my cage** . . . and there I was swimming around, **helpless** . . . and the Director wouldn't let him **devour me** so he could get a **cheap, corny happy ending** to this movie after subjecting the audience to **two hours of nauseating garbage** . . .

You mean . . .

Right! THAT, not even a **SHARK** could swallow!

145

Look...! It's the "OKRA"... the boat that helped to destroy one of "Great Whites"!

I've got news for you, Buddy! In a couple of seconds, TWO Great Whites are going to be destroyed! Mainly US!!

Remember the movie about a giant shark that took place on a quiet vacation island, and the Chief of Police couldn't get any of the Town Officials to believe that such a huge savage creature really existed until a lot of people were "JAW'D"...?

Well, **this** is the opening scene of a brand new movie about an **identical** shark, that takes place on the **same** vacation island, and the Chief of Police **still** can't get any of the Town Officials to believe that such a savage creature really exists! So **get ready**! Because that huge **shadow** moving **toward us** means that **we**, and a lot of other people, are gonna be...

JA

I'd like to thank the **Band** for their **music**... but I do think the **Choir** could have refrained from singing "...the shark has pointy teeth, dear, and he shows them, pearly white..."!

Now, "Miss Amnesty" will cut the ribbon officially opening this modern hotel that features everything a hotel on the ocean could possibly need... Dining Room, Lounges, Bar, Laundromat, Suana, Gymnasium, Restaurant, Hospital, Intensive Care Unit, Blood Bank, Shark Bite Center—

Whew! I just got here! I'm sorry that I'm late... but I had to change my clothes!

Boy, I sure wish you'd changed your **expression**!

If I'd done that, I'd've been a **DAY** late instead of an **hour** late! Did I miss anything??

The Amnesty Band **played**, the Amnesty Choir **sang**, "Miss Amnesty" **cut** the ribbon, and Mayor Fawn made a **speech**!

Yeah, but did I **MISS** anything?

PLAYING IT FOR SHARK VALUE AGAIN DEPT.

W'D, TOO

Hey, Chief! There's a **big cruiser** drifting in the **channel!** Do you want me to **go out there** and **bring it in?**

Yeah! **You're** the **Marine Cop** around here! I don't know **anything** at all about this **nautical stuff**...!

Okay! Cast off the **bow-line!** Now cast off the line that's **NOT** the bow-line! Now cast off the line that's **NEITHER** of the other two lines!

I **envy** you! You **really know** your **Seamanship!!**

There's that **new girl on the island!** Why don't you **ask** her to go sailing?

Ahhhhh! She's got boobs as big as sparrows!

Why do you always **say** things like that!? You have **no** respect for **feelings!!**

I didn't know sparrows had feelings!!

Myke, your Dad's **Chief of Police** around here, isn't he? Does he believe in **Capital Punishment?**

You bet! Why do you think he makes us come to this **island** every Summer!

ARTIST: MORT DRUCKER   WRITER: DICK DE BARTOLO

I just don't know what it **is!** I came to this vacation island to **escape** the **hassles** of the **city**... but even out here in the **ocean**, I **still** have this strange feeling I'm being **followed!**

Terry...? Terry...? Boy, that girl is such a **show-off!**

First she skis on **two** skis... then on **one** ski... and **now** she's off someplace skiing on **half** a ski! And without a tow boat!!

Good Lord!! Look at the size of that **fish!!** And me without a **rod and reel**...!

I know what I'll do! I'll **cook** it right here!!

147

Oh, dear! When it comes to cooking, I just don't seem to make it at all!
I start out trying to broil shark steaks, and I end up making "Person Flambé" . . . mainly ME!!
WOOOSH!
I saw the whole thing! There were these two people . . . skiing! They were having a marvelous time! Then . . . suddenly, there was this huge explosion! And all at once, I was having a marvelous time!!
You were having a marvelous time?
Yes! I'm an old lady! I—I never get to see ANYTHING on this desolate beach . . . except for boats and water-skiers off shore! That was a real treat! Such a big explosion! Such pretty flames! Such thick smoke!
I GAVE
Myke, I think I finally found a Summer job for you! We'll check on it tomorrow . . . !
I can't tomorrow, Dad! I'm going sailing!
Hey! You went sailing yesterday, and you went sailing today! It's not going to hurt you to miss one day of sailing!!
What kind of job is it, Dad?
It's a job working on a sailboat!
Come on! I hate sailing!
SUGAR O's
BREAKFAST OF FAT CHAMPIONS
YIPE!!
The old "sudden corpse" effect again, eh?
Hmmm! This body is burned to a crisp!
When are vacationers to this island gonna learn?!? You gotta go out into the sun GRADUALLY!! Otherwise, you're gonna get a real bad burn!
Dr. Elkhorn, I called you here as soon as the kids found this whale corpse! It's obviously been attacked by a huge shark!
Chief Broody . . . I am a member of the Scientific Community! To us, nothing is obvious! We deal only in facts! After examining the wounds, all I can say with any authority is . . . this whale was attacked by SOME BIG MOTHER!!
What would bring a huge shark like that into shore?
They like rhythm! Anything with a systematic beat! They're attracted to drumming . . . solid vibrations!
In that case, why call them "Great Whites"? "GREAT BLACKS" seems to fit better!!
Doctor Elkhorn, do sharks ever communicate? I mean . . . if one shark is killed, could another shark want to take revenge??
Sharks don't take things personally! However, as far as taking revenge is concerned, if I were you, I'd be very careful to avoid anyone who paid good money to see this disappointing sequel!!

Panel	Dialogue
1	**Gentlemen, we may have another shark problem!** We've got several people **missing**, and we found a **whale** that's been attacked by something **really huge!**
1	You're **not** gonna start that **"Great White Shark"** scare around here again, Chief Broody!
1	It's **no scare!** What about the **body with the SHARK'S TEETH** that I found on the beach?!?
1	C'mon! Lots of people wear shark's teeth for good luck!
1	Embedded in their **RIBS?!**
2	. . . and this is the **Town Beach!** As you can see, the **sand** is as **white** as **sugar** . . . except for the spots where it's **red** as **blood** . . . but we're **covering** those **over!**
2	What's that **man** doing up in that **tower?**
2	He's-*er*—he's looking for—*er*—icebergs!
2	**ICEBERGS?!?** Here?! In the middle of the Summer?!?
2	Remember what happened to the **Titanic?!** Who expected **ICEBERGS?!?** Chief Broody is **taking no chances!!**
3	**CLEAR THE WATER! GET OUT! DANGER! RUN FOR YOUR LIVES!**
3	What's everybody running for! Is there something in the water?!?
3	If there **is**, it **can't** be as dangerous as **Chief Broody!!** When he gets **excited**, he's a **lunatic** with his gun!
4	Foggy . . . you're a professional photographer and I value your opinion! Tell me . . .
4	This **picture** you're developing from that **underwater camera!** It **can't** be anything but a close-up of a huge **shark** shot at about **three feet**, right?
4	Well . . . it could **also** be a close-up of a **SARDINE** shot at about three **INCHES!**
4	Listen, you broken-down amateur! When I **want** your worthless opinion, I'll ask for it!
5	Can't you make this print a little clearer?
5	With all the **shark talk** you've been mouthing, I'm **afraid** to put my hand in the tray!!
6	We're glad you're **here**, Broody! We were just talking about **you** and your **outrageous behavior!**
6	Oh, yeah? Well, this **photograph** will show you I'm **not** mistaken! It's a **SHARK!!** Just like the **first** one! See the **eyes**, the **mouth**, the **plastic skin**, the **hydraulic hoses**, the **"Union Made"** label . . .
7	We're going into a **private meeting** now, Broody!
7	To **decide** my fate?
7	No, to decide **OUR** fates! After the **public** sees this **sequel**, I'm afraid we're **all through!**
7	I tell you, it's a **picture** of a shark! Go **have** your meeting! I'll wait here under this elephant's head!

I can't believe it! I've been fired! You know, honey, this is the first time in my life that I've ever been fired from a job!
Big deal! It's the first job you've ever had in your life!!
. . . And what really upsets me the most is that no one believes there's another shark out there!!
I do, dear!
Now, let's just forget about it! Let's have some fun!
What do you feel like doing?
Let's go for a dip in the ocean!
Hey, you guys wanna go sailing with me tomorrow? My Father has a couple of cases of beer . . . and he told me to take them out to the lighthouse . . . and drink 'em!
No kiddin'? Your Father REALLY said that?!?
Well, sort of! He actually said, "I don't want to see you drinking this beer!" So he'll never see me out that far!
Are you coming along tomorrow, Myke?
My parents want me to stay around the house!
It's too bad you listen to your parents so much! I was thinking of going topless!
Having just discovered that I'm an "Orphan". . . I'll pick you up at 8:00!
Can I ask you a personal question?
Sure!
Have we dated before . . . or is this the first time we're going out together? You see, in this movie, the teenagers all look alike! I don't know who's who!
I know what you mean! So far, two of us teenagers have been killed, and I still don't miss anybody!!
STOP POLLUTING OUR WATERS! DON'T LET THEM MAKE JAWS III!
You're going sailing, aren't you?!? Take me with you!!
What can an eleven-year-old kid do, when his Brother's got a very heavy date?
I can sail the boat while you're making out!
Get your life jacket! And hurry!!
Wasn't this a good idea, to drop behind the others . . . so we could be all by ourselves?!?
But now there's no wind!! How far do you think we can go?
Well . . . I was thinking of going "all the way"!
Oooh— Teena!! That feels good!! Boy . . . you're really—Yipe! —passionate, once you get— Oh!—started!
Easy with the TEETH, Teena! Try not to leave any marks! My parents get suspicious!

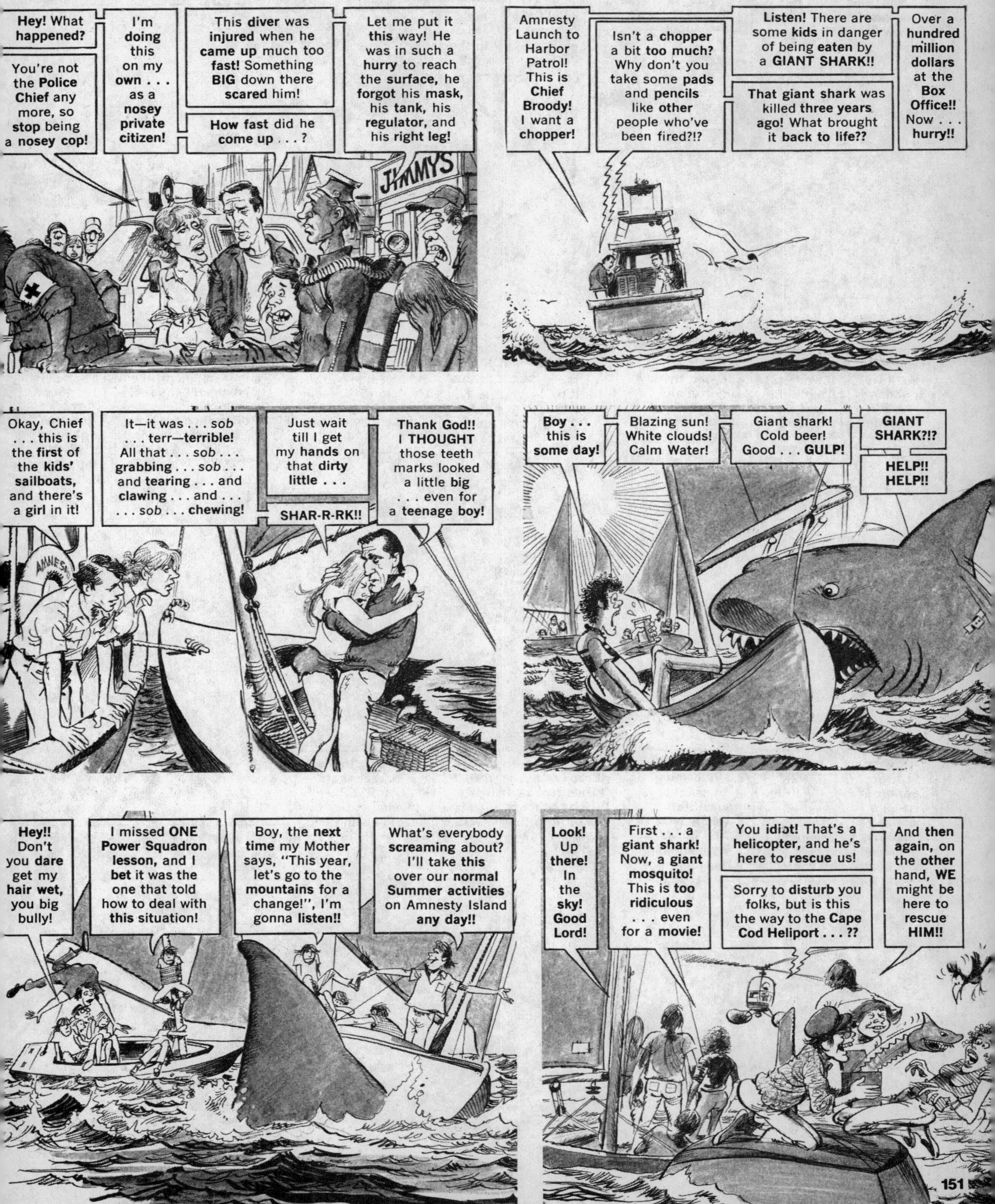

Hey! What happened?
You're not the Police Chief any more, so stop being a nosey cop!
I'm doing this on my own . . . as a nosey private citizen!
This diver was injured when he came up much too fast! Something BIG down there scared him!
How fast did he come up . . . ?
Let me put it this way! He was in such a hurry to reach the surface, he forgot his mask, his tank, his regulator, and his right leg!
JIMMYS
Amnesty Launch to Harbor Patrol! This is Chief Broody! I want a chopper!
Isn't a chopper a bit too much? Why don't you take some pads and pencils like other people who've been fired?!?
Listen! There are some kids in danger of being eaten by a GIANT SHARK!!
That giant shark was killed three years ago! What brought it back to life??
Over a hundred million dollars at the Box Office!! Now . . . hurry!!
Okay, Chief . . . this is the first of the kids' sailboats, and there's a girl in it!
It—it was . . . sob . . . terr—terrible! All that . . . sob . . . grabbing . . . sob . . . and tearing . . . and clawing . . . and . . . . . . sob . . . chewing!
Just wait till I get my hands on that dirty little . . .
SHAR-R-RK!!
Thank God!! I THOUGHT those teeth marks looked a little big . . . even for a teenage boy!
Boy . . . this is some day!
Blazing sun! White clouds! Calm Water!
Giant shark! Cold beer! Good . . . GULP!
GIANT SHARK?!?
HELP!! HELP!!
Hey!! Don't you dare get my hair wet, you big bully!
I missed ONE Power Squadron lesson, and I bet it was the one that told how to deal with this situation!
Boy, the next time my Mother says, "This year, let's go to the mountains for a change!", I'm gonna listen!!
What's everybody screaming about? I'll take this over our normal Summer activities on Amnesty Island any day!!
Look! Up there! In the sky! Good Lord!
First . . . a giant shark! Now, a giant mosquito! This is too ridiculous . . . even for a movie!
You idiot! That's a helicopter, and he's here to rescue us!
Sorry to disturb you folks, but is this the way to the Cape Cod Heliport . . . ??
And then again, on the other hand, WE might be here to rescue HIM!!

Look! The shark's attacking the helicopter!
I've heard of FLYING FISH . . . but this is ridiculous!
Let's head for the lighthouse!
Why? If it goes after people in boats and planes . . . what makes you think we'll be safe in a lighthouse?!
Nathan's
3
THUMP! THUMP! THUMP!
Okay, now let's not all go to pieces! Things will get better!
Oh, yeah! That's what YOU think!
Oh, no! Don't tell me you've spotted a second shark!!
Worse! We lost the BEER!!
Let's all paddle! We'll try to land at Tuxedo Junction!
But what if we miss?
That's the last bit of land!
No, it isn't! There's land beyond that! Unfortunately, it's 8,000 miles beyond!
DANGER
JELLY-FISH!
Look! Sworn is drifting away from us!
I'll throw him a line!
You really like little kids, don't you . . . ?
No, I hate little kids! Why should he be eaten by the shark now?! Let him suffer to the end of the movie, like the rest of us!!
C'mon! Let's play a game to keep our minds off the danger! Let's see who can guess the difference between THIS NEW movie . . . and the FIRST "JAW'D" movie?!?
You can't fool me! That's one of those "trick" questions! There IS NO difference!
Wait! I hear a motor! It—it's coming this way! It could be a boat!
Yeah, and it could be a SHARK!!
Who ever heard of a shark with a motor?!
If you were EVER going to ask that question . . . this is NOT the movie to ask that question in!
It IS a boat, and Chief Broody's at the wheel!! He's real smart! He's going to try to smash right into that shark!
The only trouble is, that shark is SMARTER! He's moving out of the way . . . but fast!!
CRASH!
POLICE

Hmm! Missed the shark completely! But I sure scared the heck out of this island!
It's okay, kids!
I'm all right!
HE'S all right!? He's high and dry on an island . . . while we're out here with a giant shark!! Of course, he's all right!!
I'm going to let out this grappling hook! Pull it over and attach it to your boats! Then, I'll haul you all over here with me!
Then we'll ALL be trapped on this deserted island!
Yeah? Then what?!?
The hook is stuck!
I'm gonna haul it back up!!
That's why he's Chief of the LAND police!
Y'know, so far, THREE of us have been eaten by that horrible shark!
Gee, am I one of the three? I REALLY have lost track of the teenagers in this movie!
Look! The hook has pulled up the underwater cable line that brings all the electricity to our island from the mainland!
Hey—Chief Broody must be going crazy! Now he's hitting the power line with a paddle!
I wonder what the power line did wrong?!?
He's really into heavy punishment, isn't he?
No—he's doing that to attract the shark!
But . . . how does he know if the shark is AC or DC?!
WAK!
Wow!! What a "shock" ending!
It looks like Chief Broody made it all right!
That's good news for the Broody family, but bad news for US!!
How come . . . ?
I don't think I could survive "JAW'D III"!!
Well, Broody, you killed the giant shark . . . and you saved the lives of five . . . maybe six teenagers! WHICH five or six . . . we may NEVER KNOW!
. . . And you're here to apologize and give me back my job!!
No . . . I'm here to tell you that you're WANTED in TEN STATES!! Because when you sacrificed that power cable, you caused a TOTAL BLACKOUT of the entire Northeast, which resulted in the loss of HUNDREDS of lives and MILLIONS of dollars in property damage!!
AMITY I
AMITY SOUND
CROTON ON HUDSON
NORTHPORT
PORT JEFFERSON
HUNTINGTON
HICKSVILLE
MINEOLA
BABYLON
NEWARK
OCEAN

IT'S STALLONE RANGER! DEPT.

For years, Hollywood made movies about the Fight Game that were loaded with clichés. Recently, however, instead of bringing back another one of those "Joe Palooka" pictures, they made a brand new type movie about the Fight Game... loaded with brand new clichés. You'll see what we mean in this version of

ROC

Hey, Rockhead! You are one lousy fighter!

Oh, yeah? Know what I'm gonna do? I'm gonna get a shot at the Champ!

The only way you'll get a shot at the Champ is if you buy a GUN!

LOOK at me! I'm a loser!

If you put on some makeup, bought some nice clothes and went to Charm School, you know what you'd be...?

Yeah! Wasting my time!

My Sister's got no social life! I see her sitting at home every night.. watching TV!

What kind of social life YOU got... sitting at home every night watching your Sister while she's watching TV?!?

I... Appalling Greed... will stage a Championship Fight on July Fourth to celebrate Independence Day!

Why Independence Day...??

'Cause I am gonna separate some Honky's head from his Honky body!

This movie shows what can happen to an underdog who keeps his faith and fights valiantly against tremendous odds!

You mean he wins in the end?

No, he gets his brains beaten out!

KHEAD

ARTIST: MORT DRUCKER

WRITER: STAN HART

Hey, Rockhead! You're out of shape! You gotta give up smoking!

Aw, do I have to?!

Well, at least while you're in the ring!!

Y'know, you goldfish are my only friends...

...but I'm afraid YOU'RE out of shape, too...

...'cause every time I take you out for a walk, you pass out before we're halfway down the block!

Gee, I'm lonely!... I had visitors walkin' in an' outta here all the time! But the place got so filthy, they don' come no more! They got too much self-respect!

Can you imagine...?! Bein' snubbed by ROACHES?!

Hey... whaddya say we talk, huh?

I'd... I'd rather not! I'm too shy!

Is that why you got your head in the birdcage?

Yeah! And at the same time, I'm havin' my HAIR frosted!

155

Panel 1:
- Listen, I'm warnin' you! You better pay Greaso The Loanshark the money you owe him... or ELSE...!
- Aw, c'mon! You... you wouldn't hurt me!
- You say that 'cause I'm too nice a guy??
- No, I say that 'cause I've seen you fight!

Panel 2:
- Nicky, why'd you give my locker t' someone else, huh?
- 'Cause you're through around here, Rockhead!
- Huh? Whaddya mean...?
- You make me sick! You coulda BEEN somethin' if you'd've worked hard! Now, you're nothin' but a BUM!
- An' if I'd've lived clean an' worked really hard, what would I be...?
- A TIRED bum!!

Panel 3:
- Wanna go to the Basketball Game wit' me, Atrium?
- No... I'm busy tonight!
- Oh? Whatcha doin'...?
- Readin'!
- Oh...? Whatcha readin'?
- "Do Not Remove This Tag Under Penalty Of Law"!
- I'll wait till the movie comes out!

Panel 4:
- Boy, I admire the Champ! I'd like to BE like him!
- What in heck for?
- Well, like, when I fight, I get all bruised up!
- Doesn't he...?
- Yeah, but when HE's black and blue, who can tell?

Panel 5:
- So the Challenger pulled out of the fight, eh? Well, I got a great idea! Listen, can you dig giving an underdog a shot at the Title?
- No...!
- Can you dig this event as a chance for an unknown to have all his dreams come true?
- No...!
- Can you dig this picture ending here and now... cause nothing's gonna happen?
- It'll be "The Fight Of The Century"!

Panel 6:
- Okay, let's look through this book and find somebody ethnic who'll fit in with the theme of the event...
- How about "The Jabbing Jew"? Or him? "The Mighty Mick"? Or "The Clobbering Kraut"?
- How about... "Cheese Danish"? Or... "Spanish Omelet"? Or... "Black Coffee"?
- Idiot! You're reading the menu from the Diner!

156

Okay, here's the one I want! "The Italian Stallion"! He must be called that because of his BUILD!
I know him! That's a typo! Actually, he's called "The Italian Scallion" . . . because of his BREATH!
Hey, Rockhead! If you get me a part time job with Greaso The Loanshark, you will go out with my Sister!
An' if I get you a FULL TIME job wit' him . . .?
Then I won't make you go out with her!
I want you should go out with Rockhead!
No, Bawly! He wants what all the other guys want!
Sure . . . but the difference is . . . he forgets what it IS!
No . . . I refuse!!
This is some Thanksgiving Day Party!! You know what you can do?! You can t'row the damn turkey out the window for all I care!!
I meant THIS turkey . . . not THAT turkey!!
CRASH!
Hey, Atrium! How about goin' out wit me, huh . . .?
She ain't answering, Bawly! I don't think she likes me!
Keep after her!
Sure she does! You got a certain quality she loves!
C'mon, will you! I'm stupid, I'm a slob and I got no future! What kinda quality have I got?
Honesty . . .!!
My Fadder tol' me t' always use my brawn . . . 'cause I got a great body, but no brains!
My Father told me to use my brains . . . because my body is nothing!
Hey, we make a great team! Imagine if we had a baby an' he had your brains an' my body?!?
With our luck, he'd have YOUR brains and MY body!
Ahhh, so what! That didn't stop Sonny Bono!
Nobody wants to fight me 'cause I'm a lefty! I never amounted to much 'cause nobody gave me a chance!
Could your clumsiness have any-thing to do with it?
I'm not Clumsy! This ice is slippery!
But we're not on the ice anymore!

You live here all alone?!?
That you needed some help to get this place as filthy as it is!
I don't think I should stay, but somehow, I can't seem to leave!
No . . . I'm stuck here in your couch . . . because of this broken spring!
Sure!! Wha'd ya think?
C'mon, now! Why don' you relax?
You're turned on by my looks, huh?
Hold still! Let me take off your glasses!
Oh, that's such a cliché! You wanna see if I'm pretty!
No, I DON'T want you to see where my hands are going!
Please! Don't start anything! I have a confession to make! I'm 30 years old and still a virgin!
That must be tough!
It's only been tough the last 20 years!
Please! I . . . I never kissed a man before!
What HAVE you kissed?
Every animal in the pet shop . . .
You'll never know the difference!
Rockhead . . . how would you like to fight the Champ . . . Appalling Greed?
Are you kiddin'?! I ain't good enough t'—oops!
You're perfect!! You'll get 150 grand for doing what you just did!
What'd I just do??
Fall on your face!
Will he hit me a lot?!?
My guess would be . . . just once!
I'd like to manage you for the big fight, my boy!
Why . . . ?
'Cause I've always treated you like a Father would!
What? You t'row my stuff in the street . . . you yell at me in front of everyone . . . you make me feel like a stupid useless little kid!
See! I told you I treat you like a Father would!
Gotta start my training! Now, let's see this schedule I gotta keep . . .
4:00 A.M. Wake up and get out of bed!
4:05 A.M. Crack 8 raw eggs into a glass!
4:10 A.M. Swallow the 8 raw eggs . . .
EGGS
4:12 A.M. . . . vomit . . .

Panel 1:
- Rockhead tell us... in training for the Championship fight, why do you hit raw meat?!?
- Because hitting raw FISH makes my hands smell! It also toughens me up, and gets me used to the sight of blood!
- I see! So when your opponent gets gory, it won't upset you!
- No, so when I get gory, it won't upset me!!
- Besides, they pay me t'ree bucks an hour! I'm cheaper den usin' CHEMICAL MEAT-TENDERIZERS!

THUD!

Panel 2:
- Rockhead, wanna go inside and you-know-what...?
- I—I can't! My manager tol' me not to mess aroun' wit' girls 'cause I'm IN TRAINING!
- To be a Champ... or to be a Priest?!

Panel 3:
- I don' want my Sister makin' out wit' some bum who won't even get me a job!!
- This house isn't big enough for both Bawly and me anymore! How do you feel about living together...?
- Nahh! Bawly snores!
- I mean with ME!!

CRASH!

Panel 4:
- I don't think I can beat him, Atrium! All I wanna do is go the distance!
- You—you mean the distance in the fight??
- No, the distance between here an Sydney, Australia!

Panel 5:
- Hey! What a smart Promoter you are, Champ... comin' into the ring dressed as The Father of our Country!
- Glad you like it, MOTHER!!
- Gee... and you were even kind enough to figure ME in on it!

Panel 6:
- Hit me all you want to, Champ! That's my "Plan A"... where you tire yourself out!
- But I never get tired!
- Well... then... I'll immediately switch to "Plan B"... where you KILL ME!!

I COULD'A BEEN A CONTENDER

Panel 7:
- Hey... do you think he has a chance?
- Against the Champ? Absolutely not!!
- I'm not talking about this phony movie fight! I mean, do you think he has a chance of winning The Academy Award??
- Against Peter Finch?? Absolutely not!!

159

Both your eyes are shut tight! At least that's ONE lucky thing . . . !
What's lucky about that?
Now you can't see your nose is broken!
This round, I give him and uppercut in the ribs, a hook in the sirloin and a jab in the brisket!
Geez, I told you you were sparring with those sides of beef too much!
ROUND
8
I . . . I gotta get up! An' . . . an' I only got ten seconds to do it!
Take your time! Don't you know that in all Fight Pictures, it takes the Referee a full two minutes to count to ten?!?
This is the bloodiest, most gruesome encounter I've seen since last Thursday!!
What happened last Thursday?
The Philadelphia Flyers played The New York Rangers in a hockey game!!
We have a split decision!
The Judges have awarded 15 points for Rockhead . . .
18 points for the Champ . . .
. . . and 25 points for the Make-Up Man!!
Atrium, I love you! Will ya marry me?
Oh . . . yes! Yes! I will Rockhead!
Isn't that warm and wonderful! An under-dog sees his dreams come true, marries the girl and lives happily ever after!!
Oh, yeah? I'm not so sure! Look . . .
Stand up. Rockhead! Don't slouch! Stop mumbling when you talk! Tie your robe! Wash your hands and face and show me they're clean! If they're not, back you go to the bathroom and do it all over again! Now, the first thing—
Hey, le'me get MY licks in, Atrium, in as much as I'm gonna live wit' you! Now, I need a new car, an' a new suit, an' . . .